I0580346

# ALSO BY RUSSELL NOHELTY

**THE OBSIDIAN SPINDLE SAGA**
The Sleeping Beauty
The Wicked Witch
The Fairy Queen
The Red Rider
**THE GODVERSE CHRONICLES**
And Death Followed Behind Her
And Doom Followed Behind Her
And Ruin Followed Behind Her
And Hell Followed Behind Her
And Conquest Followed Behind Them
And Darkness Followed Behind Her
And Chaos Followed Behind Them
Katrina Hates the Dead
Pixie Dust
**OTHER NOVEL WORK**
My Father Didn't Kill Himself
Sorry for Existing
Gumshoes: The Case of Madison's Father
The Invasion Saga
The Vessel
Worst Thing in the Universe
The Void Calls Us Home
The Marked Ones
**OTHER ILLUSTRATED WORK**
The Little Bird and the Little Worm
Ichabod Jones: Monster Hunter
Gherkin Boy
**www.russellnohelty.com**

# WHITE RABBIT

## Book 1 of the Wonderland duology

By:

Russell Nohelty

Edited by:

Jonas Saul

Proofread by:

Lily Luchesi

Toni Cox

Cover by:

Paramita Bhattacharjee

# CHAPTER ONE

*Wonderland.*

Dark. Grimy. Unsavory.

It didn't use to be this way. It used to be fun. Hell, it was downright enjoyable once upon a time, back when the Red Queen had her way.

Or at least that's what they said since I was a kid.

Back when the Red Queen ran things, everybody was happy. Yeah, everybody was high as a kite all the time, seeing shit that didn't exist, and that wasn't ideal, but at least it was a gay old time. People didn't care about mortgages, drug addiction, or any of the million fucking things that popped up after she was ousted from office during The Lory Coup three decades ago.

Because of that coup, I chased down criminals selling knockoff versions of the Queen's goofy juice, White Rabbit. The city council tried to suppress it, but Rabbit kept flaring up like herpes every couple of months. They can't get rid of it because people want it.

Who wouldn't?

People were desperate to forget their shitty lives, and White Rabbit was a pretty good way to do it—no, an excellent way to do it. Citizens tried getting their fix from LSD, weed, and magic mushrooms, but it wasn't the same. There's nothing like the rush of Rabbit. With Rabbit, everything else in your life melted away. When you were on Rabbit, you knew your best friend was a flamingo, and you didn't care. You just believed. You were one with the weirdness.

That's what made it so special. That's why everybody chased Rabbit, from housewives to senators to NARCO officers and everybody in between. It transported you to a magical place. A place nothing like the shithole Wonderland became after the fall of the Red Queen.

Sure. Now we had justice. Now we had order. Now we had laws. But who the fuck needed laws when you could have tea with a rabbit and a walrus? Who the fuck needed justice when you could smoke opium with a caterpillar?

Fucking nobody. That's who. That's why Rabbit's never gone off the market. Sure, it's ebbed and flowed over the years. When shit was good, there was little need for it, but more often than not, shit was bad. That's when the people of Wonderland needed Rabbit the most. Recently, it's all gone to pot, which is why we've seen the biggest surge of Rabbit since the old days.

It's why I sat outside a shitty alley in the first place, in an unmarked car, waiting for a hog-nosed kid with a bullring to wave me forward.

*Hog-nose.*

He was gonna regret that in the future. Most morphers picked something pretty when they mutilated themselves, like a kitty or a hamster, something people wanted to pet, not kill and eat. Something that brought the warm fuzzies to the cockles of your stomach. Hog morphers were never that popular in Wonderland, except as a big "fuck you" to the system that worshiped cute.

Also, becoming a hog was cheap, and cheap wasn't sexy. You could turn into a hog for a few grand. Even back-alley surgeons had little problem warping people into hogs.

The guy at the end of the block, the drug dealer I was waiting for, he became a bunny, whiskers and all. It cost a good fifty thousand to turn into a bunny, and that's on the low end. High-quality fur could set you back thousands more. The better the quality, the higher the cost. Rabbits, flamingos, walruses, you didn't see them often—at least not good ones—because everybody wanted to be them. Supply and demand was a bitch, and who had that kind of money except the filthy rich?

Nobody I came across on the regular. But mutilating yourself was still cheaper than Rabbit. If you wanted to get the pure strain of the good stuff, well, you better have a trust fund. Knock-off versions could be bought cheap, but they were also likely to kill you.

That's why I was hanging out in this dark alley in the first place. Twenty-three have died so far from a new strain of Rabbit. It's supposed to get you higher than a motherfucker—once. Then it killed you. For some people, once was all they needed. Some people, they'd take the ecstasy of Wonderland, true Wonderland, once in their life if it meant they would die blissfully happy. For most, it's the first happiness they have felt since the coup.

The pig-nosed lookout knocked on my car window. "You got exact change, bitch?"

I clenched my fist. I couldn't deck him. He was testing me. Hog-nose would insult me until I either screamed and lashed out, or he was satisfied I was desperate and docile enough to meet the dealer.

"Y-y-y-y-es," I muttered. The timider I sounded, the quicker he would be satisfied.

The pig snorted. "That's good. You know, we got some time. How about you suck on my cock while you wait?"

I shook my head. "I can't—my husband—"

"The fuck I care about him? He don't hafta know. He don't hafta know shit. He know you on the Rabbit, bitch? Nah, you do it on the down-low, and you can suck me off on the down-low, too. And if he tried to do something …" He tapped his gun on my driver's side door. "Then I'll handle it."

He unzipped his pants. I pressed my hand on my stick shift. There was a lot I would do for the NARCOs, but swallowing cock wasn't one of them. Lucky for me, the car in front of me drove away, and the bunny snapped his fingers.

"Looks like you missed out, ho. The bunny will see you now."

I wanted so badly to rip off his dick as I pulled forward, but I was on the job. I would have to come back later and beat him senseless. That was the good thing about being a NARCO; they let you do whatever the fuck you wanted as long as it didn't interfere with a sting operation.

# CHAPTER TWO

I inched my car forward. The closer I came to the bunny, the more impressive his transformation became to me. Most morphers used coarse, tight hair and matted it on in clumps to save on cost, but this bunny was special. This bunny drilled plugs right into his skin. That's at least a hundred grand on the low end, and this bunny didn't seem like he did anything low end. Crime definitely paid in Wonderland, at least for some people.

"What you want?" the bunny asked.

"Three bottles."

The bunny glared at me. His eyes, completely black, glinted in the streetlight. The level of detail in his transformation was astounding. He scratched his fingers together. "The money. Five hundred dollars."

"That's steep."

"You want the best. The real OG shit. I'm the only place that has it."

"That's the real? The pure?"

The bunny wiggled his nose. "Yeah. You heard me. The real shit."

There was no way it was the real stuff. The real stuff would have been ten times more than that, but I didn't complain. I just needed proof of the transfer for the bust.

I pulled five hundred dollars out of a yellow envelope and handed it to him. "Give it to me."

My earpiece crackled with the gruff voice of my partner. "Wait for it."

The bunny's ear twitched. "What was that?"

Fuck. *I was found.* Goddamn it, Captain. Couldn't you keep your fucking mouth shut for two seconds? "Nothing. I just heard the wind. It does funny shit to your mind."

The bunny latched onto the door handle. "Get out the car."

I pressed down on the lock. "That's all right. I'm not—"

The bunny lunged inside the window before I could roll it up. His talons clawed at my shirt. "Come here!"

"Get off me. Get off me!"

In the struggle, the earpiece tumbled out of my ear. *Fuck.*

"She's a rat!"

I pulled my earpiece close to my mouth. "It's over. Come in *now!*"

A dozen floodlights blinded the alley. The bunny spun on his heels. "Shit! It's a raid. Scatter!"

The bunny disappeared into an alley. Protocol said to wait for backup before pursuing a perp, but fuck protocol. I had a job to do, even if it killed me.

Hell, especially if it killed me.

I chased the bunny down into a tight alley. The gun slid out of my holster in rhythm with my strides. My breath eased. My eyes narrowed. I focused on my heartbeat. My ability to calm myself even in the worst situations was one reason I made detective after two years, even if it was only on the vice squad. I never let my emotions get the better of me. I maintained control no matter the danger.

I homed in on the pitter-patter of the bunny's feet. They turned right, then left. I glided around the corners to track him, his tiny steps matched by my long, arched ones. With every step, I gained on him. In thirty more seconds, I would be on his heels.

*Left. Right. Left.* He was a rat in a maze with no way out. I caught the corner of his ear after another two turns. I smelled his sweaty fur in another.

*Right. Right. Left. Right. Left.*

I halted before the next corner and tilted my head out, hidden by the darkness of the night. The bunny wandered down the alley, scared and alone. I took another breath. "Put your hands on the wall."

He heaved, barely able to speak. "You'll never get me!"

"Idiot, I've already gotten you."

"You have no idea—"

I stepped out of the shadows, gun drawn. "Do you have any clue how many of you I track down each year?"

He placed his knees on the ground, sucking wind. I almost felt bad for him. That soft, cuddly fur on his face was going to be very popular in prison. He was gonna make some bull very, very happy.

"I'm not gonna go to prison. I can't. She'll kill me."

I let my eye slip for a second. I didn't see him cup a bottle of Rabbit in his hand. I didn't see his shoulder jerk. I didn't see the bottle until it smashed into my face.

He ran.

My eyes blurred. "Stop! Stop!"

I shot into the air. Again. And again. A knee hit the ground. Then, a head. Mine wasn't far behind.

The world floated away and returned in hyper color. Flamingos danced in the street. Wrought-iron gates transformed into Twizzlers. Every thought that weighed me down floated away.

I'd never been to Wonderland before, and now that I had, I never wanted to leave.

# CHAPTER THREE

I spent three weeks in a blissful, foggy haze, dozing in and out of consciousness long enough to repeatedly witness doctors pulling me back from the brink of death. My heart stopped six times that first night. They would have pronounced me dead were it not for my partner Dormouse threatening to kill them if I died.

I didn't care, though, because I was high on Rabbit.

Inside my dreams, I finally understood the blissful splendor of Wonderland. Everything was bright and cheerful. Decks of cards painted buildings, and smiling gorillas looked after me with their oversized stethoscopes and charts. During fits of consciousness, funny dodo birds squawked at me while the heart monitor danced around the room singing show tunes.

Even Dormouse, usually tall, stoic, and broad, took on a new look like a diminutive mouse in a bellhop uniform. I lived in Wonderland my whole life and only heard the tales of its glory years, back when everybody drank Rabbit. Now, in my flurry of pure ecstasy, I understood people's wistful accounts of the place.

By the time I was born into the world, White Rabbit had been out of the water system for three years, and the Queen was already well into her one thousand consecutive life sentences for crimes against the realm.

Now that I had a taste of Rabbit, though, I had to ask, was what she did so bad?

Yes, I knew that the economic system collapsed under her reign, and the Queen lopped off people's heads at the drop of a hat, but was Wonderland any better now? Are diplomatic relations with Emerald City any better than a generation ago? Not by any discernible measure.

Now, power rests with a new group, one more dower and drab than the Red Queen and without her flare for the dramatic. They exhibited the same bloodlust, though. The city council wrestled with different demons than the Red Queen, but they were demons nonetheless.

The doctors kept me in the hospital under observation for two more weeks after I finally stopped the hallucinations. Those were the worst weeks of my life. The withdrawal brutalized my body like nothing I'd ever felt. Cold sweats and hot flashes crashed upon me simultaneously. Needles pricked through every inch of my flesh. The nurses locked my arms and legs in place so I couldn't run screaming out a window. If I had access to even the dullest knife, I would have cut my jugular to avoid the pain.

Yet, that wasn't the worst part. The worst part came after I regained my senses.

Dormouse visited me often in the hospital. Sometimes he was a bellhop with a squeaky voice and whiskers. Other times he was the friend I remember, deliberate and kind. Either way, he brought comfort to my wounded mind in the worst moments of my life. It wasn't until I regained my senses and faculties that he told me of my new reality.

"How much do you remember about that night?" he asked, crouched at my bedside.

"Not much. I chased a perp down an alley. He threw Rabbit in my face. I hit him twice. I know that. He went down. Then I went down."

Dormouse took a deep breath. "You got somebody, but it wasn't the bunny."

I shot up in bed. "Of course it was. There was nobody else in that alley."

Dormouse slid a folder out of his jacket. He showed me the crime scene photos of a little kid bleeding out over the street. "There was a kid…"

I clasped my mouth. My eyes rolled back in my head, and I fought to remain conscious. "I couldn't. That couldn't…"

Dormouse placed his free hand on mine. "I know this is a lot to process. I waited until you were better, but you need to know. They're calling for your head."

I scrambled for a remote to turn on the news before I realized there wasn't a TV in my room.

Dormouse didn't blink. "I asked them to remove the television for your sanity. I thought it would be best. I didn't want you to see the truth until you were better."

"Oh, you thought it would be best? I'm a goddamn adult, Dormouse, and I can take care of myself. Get me a fucking television."

The ruckus drove two NARCO officers into the room, clad in their iconic black pinstripe uniforms. "Is there a problem in here?" one demanded brusquely.

Dormouse held up his arm. "It's okay, Officers. Nothing to see here. Go back to your post."

The officers nodded and shuffled back outside, taking positions on each side of the door.

"Are they there for my protection?" I asked. "Or am I a prisoner?"

"You'll be brought in for questioning once you are well. Everybody is on your side on this. We know what you've been through. You're a good NARCO. You'll be back on active duty in no time."

Active duty, as if I gave a shit about that. I cared about the fact that I killed a little kid. How could I live with myself for one more second? All I wanted was to escape into the world of Wonderland, where everything is perfect, forever.

Eventually, though, the doctors ran out of tests, and there was nothing left for me except the release papers. Once the doctor signed me out, the two officers guarding the door wasted no time shackling me.

"You are being arrested for the crime of murder. You will have access to an attorney should you need one. Do not speak unless spoken to for any reason. You have forfeited your right to freedom until you are deemed innocent by a tribunal."

The flashbulbs started before I even stepped my first foot out of the hospital. Lines of picketers screamed as we made our way into the NARCO van.

I had never been called such vile things. At least not all at once. The occasional criminal deemed me a "cunt" or a "bitch," but never in thousand-person choruses. I struggled to breathe in the thick wave of hatred. Their vitriol punched me in the gut and sapped all my air. It wasn't until I was safe inside the NARCO van that I gained it back again, though I could still hear them shouting, and some of them threw rotten food as we sped off.

# CHAPTER FOUR

They brought me to trial a month later. Three surly NARCO captains from around the city stood in judgment over me. "Alice Liddell. This tribunal is convened to find the truth behind the shooting of Timothy Leary, aged ten, on the night of April seventeenth. How do you respond to these charges?"

I glanced at my NARCO-appointed attorney. He excelled at exonerating officers. That was his reputation. He coached me for a week straight before the trial. He taught me how to carry myself and forced me to practice every inch of my testimony. We rehearsed for six hours a day, every day.

I wanted to admit my guilt. I felt guilty—I *was* guilty—but he told me not to throw away my life no matter what I thought.

"The truth is," he said, "you still have a lot to do in the world. You can still do a lot of good. Just because you feel guilty doesn't mean you are guilty."

I sat on the witness stand at criminal trials dozens of times, looking into the cold, dead eyes of the worst scum on the Earth, wondering why they didn't confess, wondering how they could let their crimes fester inside of them. Now I knew. It was simple fear. Fear of losing everything. Fear of being locked away. When everything else is stripped away, we aren't much more than animals, and animals, at their basest instincts, want to survive.

"Miss Liddell," the judge said. "How do you respond to the charges levied against you?"

"Innocent, Your Honors."

The head of the tribunal jotted it down in her notes. "It's not required to call us Honor. We aren't judges."

I looked up at them. "But you will judge me, right?"

"We will."

"Then you are judges in my eyes, Your Honor."

I saw the corner of her mouth turn up. I made an impression. That was the most important thing, my attorney told me, to make an impression.

"The more they humanize you," he told me, "the better your chances for acquittal. They hold your future in their hands. Do everything in your power to charm them."

The trial lasted four days, but it felt like an eternity. They asked me every question imaginable, from my childhood to my work record, to the events of the night I shot a kid.

Those words stuck with me. I shot an innocent kid. It didn't matter if I did it by accident or even if I was justified. I still shot him. He died because of me. They called his family to the stand on the third day. That was the hardest part.

"He was a sweet boy," his mother said from the stand. "He just loved playing so much. He wanted to be a NARCO officer. He wanted to help people."

She burst down crying on the stand for ten minutes. My heart ached for her. I wanted to reach out, but I knew I couldn't. I'd done my damage. I couldn't heal it. It took everything in my power to stop from changing my plea to guilty right then and there.

Eventually, it was over. The judges smiled a grim smile and scattered into the ether to deliberate. My attorney walked me into the hallway, shackles dragging behind me like a tail, and patted my back.

"You did good in there. You showed them you were a person. People make mistakes. Monsters kill people, but people make mistakes. Say it."

"Monsters kill people."

"That's not—"

"I know what you meant. Just leave me alone, all right?"

I sat on the bench outside the court building, alone, except for the two silent officers flanking me on each side. And I thought. I had a long time to think about my life. It's all I did those days; think about my life and all the choices that brought me here. Valedictorian. Magna Cum Laude. First in my class at NARCO Academy. Was it really worth it? Was it worth all the hard work just so I could end up here, with only a shitty apartment to show for it and not nearly enough money in the bank? Was any of this really worth it?

Of course, I knew the answer to that question. It wasn't. I should have been a simple farmer, a seamstress, or opened a little muffler shop outside Wonderland with my sister. I would have been happier, I think, if I had been born dumber, with less ambition. I wouldn't have been here, right now, facing God knows what punishment, that's for sure. The tribunal could tell me anything, from letting me off the hook, sentencing me to prison, cutting off my head, or anything between. Honestly, I would welcome having my head cut off at this point. At least then it would be over.

The tribunal deliberated for seven hours. Seven of the longest hours of my life, yet I didn't want them to end. I knew once I sat in that courtroom again, the rest of my life would be decided for me.

"It's okay," my lawyer told me. "The longer they deliberate, the better."

"Better for whom?" Not better for the family whose boy I shot. They stared daggers into my back throughout the whole trial. Silent and judging. Even if I got off, did I think I could go back onto the force? Would anybody respect me again? Would anybody let me do my job? Could I walk down the street without getting looks and stares? Would I be safe anywhere?

Eventually, the tribunal called me back into the courtroom. "Please rise," a gruff bailiff shouted. "This tribunal is now in session."

My attorney and I stood as the three stone-faced members of the tribunal shuffled inside and took their seats. The woman in the center spoke for the group. "We have deliberated long about this matter. On the one hand, a child is dead, and there is nothing we can do to ease that pain for the family or the community. On the other, there is the matter of the facts at hand and whether you were justified in shooting your gun at an escaping perpetrator."

She cleared her throat. "This has given us pause because while it was not good judgment by any matter, it was this department who trained you to use your gun and released you into the world, and as such, it must take some responsibility as well.

"And yet, one cannot punish an institution with jail time or any other punishment which can be inflicted onto a person. This brings us back to you, Alice Liddell, and what should be done with you."

The woman looked to each side of herself and received the slightest of nods from each other member. "It is of our opinion that you were within your judgment as a NARCO officer to discharge your weapon at an escaping perpetrator. Therefore, we find you innocent on the charges presented to you."

The courtroom gasped.

I gasped.

My knees buckled.

I fell to the ground.

"However," she continued, "we believe your judgment was impaired in such a way that you will be required to attend regular psychological evaluations and be remanded to desk duty until your commanding officer deems you fit for active duty. That is all. Thank you for your time."

The tribunal left without another word. The courtroom erupted with hisses, exclamations of anger and bitterness. The seated constituents rose out of their seats and rushed me in a wave. A cadre of officers ran into the room to subdue them, giving my lawyer time to push me out the back entrance.

The courtroom's screams dimmed as the riotous shouts from the outside swelled. The front door to the courthouse rattled and shook with the ferocity of the city bearing down on it.

My lawyer grabbed my arms. "Listen to me. This isn't over. Just because you won in that room does not mean you won in the court of public opinion. Things are going to be bad for you for a while. You need to stay low. You need to blend in. Let this die down because it will die down. Soon, the public will be onto some other thing."

I looked up at him with a tear in my eye. "When? A day? A week? A year?"

He shook his head. "I don't know. I can't say, but it will blow over if you give it time. They will forget."

"And forgive? What about that? Will they forgive?"

"I can't promise that," he said with bitter sadness. "That's over my pay grade."

# CHAPTER FIVE

I took my phone off the ringer the first day I came home. The death threats blew up my phone on a nonstop loop. All day it was telemarketers and death threats. Even the few people who called to wish me well only did so out of pity. I didn't need anybody to tell me they were on my side. How could you be on the side of a child murderer, anyway?

There were texts and Facebook messages in the thousands by the end of the first week, but I didn't check them. I tried it once, and a bevy of nasty articles bombarded me with tales about how terrible I was and how the union had sided with another bad NARCO.

I was the poster child for everything wrong with the NARCOs. Hell, I was the poster child for everything wrong in Wonderland. Thing is, they were right. I was everything that was wrong with Wonderland. I shot a kid and got off with paid leave. I would be allowed to get back on the force. Worst yet, they allowed me to keep breathing. Meanwhile, that poor fucking family. That poor fucking family. They would never be whole again, thanks to me.

I didn't leave the house for two weeks after they brought me home. I stayed shriveled up in my comfy pants, watching reruns of bad reality shows. I knew I should leave, but I couldn't make it to the door. Every step toward freedom suffocated me.

It didn't help that protesters screamed outside my building day and night. Their screaming crashed atop my eardrums like waves. I felt bad for the other tenants in my building—I deserved it, but they didn't. Though the court proved my innocence, I still shot a child.

I pulled the trigger, and for what? So that I could stop a bad guy? It's not like stopping that bunny would prevent White Rabbit from flooding the streets. It's not like it would have changed anything. What would have been harmed by letting him go besides my ego?

But that's the trick. My ego was so massive I couldn't let him go. I had to stop him. I had to have my collar. I didn't want to look bad in front of the captain, and now here I am, looking bad in front of all of Wonderland.

"Take all the time you need," the captain told me. "You're still on administrative leave for at least a month anyway. You'll come back in due time."

Administrative leave. "Paid vacation," the boys in the precinct called it. They laughed and patted each other on the back when they got busted. It was a chance to catch up on some reading on the city's dime.

But I didn't read. Maybe I should have, but I didn't. And I'd already caught up on all the crappy movies in my house. After a week on leave, I stared blankly at the walls all day and wished for death. Moreover, I wished for another taste of White Rabbit so I could escape my pain. Those blissful moments in Wonderland were the happiest of my life.

It's not like my life was so bad, either. I always had enough to eat and drink. But, fuck, everything was always so gloomy in Wonderland. Everybody walked around pissed off all the time. The streets were dingy. Everything was covered with a thick layer of film.

On White Rabbit, though, Wonderland was a happy place. It was bright and sunny, and it smelled like candy. I'm surprised there weren't more riots when the city council took Rabbit off the streets. Probably because everybody faced withdrawals at the same time. They didn't know what to think. Wonderland Mental Hospital still has withdrawal patients there. We call them "lifers." People who couldn't deal with the real world. People who were a danger to themselves. People like my father.

Dad didn't start as a junkie. He recovered quite nicely when they took Rabbit out of the water stream, but after having my sister and me, his life descended into chaos. He couldn't handle the pressure of putting food on the table for three other people and himself. He lost it and started chasing the Rabbit. The shit they used to sell right after the purge was good. It was pure. But as the supply dissipated and the NARCOs cracked down harder on the drug dealers, Rabbit lost its purity and became junk. Dealers cut Rabbit with anything to make a buck. When the government had regulated it under the Red Queen, at least there were some standards. On the open market, anything was fair game.

I remembered Dad coming home from work reeking of booze, a twinkle in his eye from the Rabbit wearing off. Then, one day he didn't come home at all. We found him strung out three weeks later, out of his mind on Rabbit. That was the moment I decided to be a NARCO.

# CHAPTER SIX

The banging on my door started at ten a.m. I tried to get to it, but I couldn't will myself within thirty feet of it. I tried again about fifteen minutes later because the banging didn't stop, but I only got twenty feet away. I crawled and crawled my way to the door until I finally reached it, hyperventilating and wheezing, at 10:30. I pushed myself onto my hands and knees and finally turned the latch.

My sister, to her credit, was nothing if not persistent. She stood in the doorway with six bags of groceries behind her.

"Took you long enough," she said, dragging me to my feet. "Help me with these."

The hallway. I couldn't possibly look out into the hallway. The thought of stepping out of my apartment caught me with dread and anger. If I put my hand across the threshold, it would burn off.

Dinah jumped over me. "Fine. I'll do it." She grunted, grabbing two more bags as I turned back into the apartment.

I lifted myself onto my feet to join her. My breath returned once I turned away from the door. "Thank you for the food."

"Well, I assumed you wouldn't be leaving the house after the trial—not that you did before—and I didn't want you to starve to death. When did you change the locks?"

The new lock on my door was no joke. The NARCOs installed a steel reinforced door with a deadbolt. It was a real fancy one. They also installed bars on my windows so people couldn't break in from the balcony.

"After I got back. The department did it for me. Figured I could use more protection."

"Well, it's incredibly annoying. You could have told me my key wouldn't work."

"Yeah. When?"

Dinah eyeballed the phone. "When you put your phone back on the ringer."

She lunged over to the phone, but I blocked her. "No, Dinah. Don't."

"Please, what's the worst that can happen?"

I grabbed the receiver out of her hand. "Please."

She threw up her hands. "Fine. What do I know? I'm just your big sister."

"Ever shot a kid before?"

"Well, no—"

"Then let's pretend I know more about this than you."

She didn't say another word for a while. She went about putting away the groceries. She knew my cupboards better than I did. I never ate at home before the incident. I was always on the job. Greasy burgers were my staple food. Such a fucking NARCO cliché.

After she was done, Dinah walked to the window and looked down at the protestors.

"There's so many of them."

I counted my protesters every morning. Today there were less than a dozen. A week ago, there were over a hundred at all hours of the day and night. People were growing weary of me, just like my lawyer told me. "That's nothing. Day one, there were three hundred. They shut down the street."

"What do your neighbors say?"

"I don't talk to them, so I wouldn't know."

"Have you showered since you got home?"

"I'm sure I have."

She turned to me. "If you can't remember, it's been too long. Go shower. You'll feel better."

Dinah was right. I was surprised by how quickly my mood changed after a long, hot shower. It was as if all the shittiness from the past few weeks washed down the drain and swirled into nothingness.

When I came out of the bathroom, Dinah had clothes laid out for me. "Get dressed. We're going out."

The hairs on the back of my neck shot up. "No. No. I'm not…I can't." My knees crumbled inside of me. I dropped to the floor. "I can't. I can't go. I can't. I can't."

Dinah bent down next to me. "You are the strongest person I know. You fight criminals every day, and look at you. You're freaked out by a fucking door? Think about that for a second. Doesn't that seem kind of ridiculous?"

It did seem a bit ridiculous, but it didn't stop the feeling of fright that came with even looking over at the doorway.

Dinah propped me up. "Besides, you can't stay inside all the time. Eventually, you are going to run out of money and get evicted. What are you going to do then?"

"Live with you, I guess?"

She chortled. "You would hate my house. There are kids running around all the time. It's loud, it smells, and to top it off, there's no way I could live with you again. You're a complete downer."

I smiled. I couldn't remember the last time I smiled. "And you are way too cheerful."

"See? It would never work out. So how about we get you out of this house, so you can become a functional member of society again."

I took a deep breath. "Okay."

"Great. Because I don't want to come back to this neighborhood for a long time."

We sat at a café with thousands of people passing in front of us, and nobody raised an eyebrow. There were still picketers at my door, but in the real world, people seemed unfazed by my appearance. They didn't point me out. They didn't snicker. They didn't spew hatred. They didn't know me at all, it seemed.

My lawyer was right. The people of Wonderland didn't care. It's easy to rile people up for a day, maybe a week, but after a couple of months, they forget and carry on with their daily lives. It doesn't take much to turn their attention to the newest, shiniest problem.

"Quit looking over your shoulder," Dinah said after a big inhale of coffee. "Nobody's coming."

"I can't help it. If just one crazy person knew where I was…"

"Yeah, I think the only crazy person here is you."

"Then you don't know Wonderland."

"The news doesn't even cover you anymore. Nobody cares about you."

"What a lovely thought."

I had to admit, it was nice to imagine a world where nobody gave a shit about me. Nobody used to give a shit about me, and I took it for granted. All I wanted in the world was anonymity.

"So, is it as bad as you thought, coming outside?"

"It's all right, Dinah. Nice, even."

"I'll take it."

I wasn't forthcoming with the compliments, even on my most gracious days. A hint of appreciation was on par with jumping for joy and praising her as the second coming.

Dinah took another sip of coffee. "Maybe I can even get you out to the 'burbs one of these days."

She kept prattling on, but I was distracted by the large bunny ears flopping by on the street behind her. I would recognize them anywhere. They were the ears of the bunny that ruined my life. Nobody had ears like my drug dealing bunny. He didn't hide them either. He flaunted them, preened them even, as he waited for the light to change. We saw all sorts of animals outside the coffee shop. Most of them couldn't afford the surgeries necessary to implant new hair all over their body or reform their bones to look like animals. They often wore masks to cover the uneven patchwork growing around their bodies.

After their transformation, animals looked normal—well, normal for Wonderland. Depending on how much you spent on doctors and materials, you could look like a cheap knockoff puppet or a beautifully handcrafted plush. Very few looked like the real thing. That was a cost so high almost nobody reached it. You would have to mortgage your mansion a couple of times to even come close.

Still, there he was, the bunny, in the flesh, just a couple of feet from me. I could have reached out and bashed his head into the sidewalk.

"Hey!" Dinah shouted. "Are you listening to me?"

"No." The light changed, and I hopped up to follow the rabbit. "I have to go."

# CHAPTER SEVEN

I followed the bunny for sixteen blocks as he weaved through the crowded alleys of Wonderland. It was easy to keep tabs on him, what with the massive ears and all. I wondered whether his bosses hated his ostentatiousness or if they loved that he stood out everywhere he went. After all, the bunny would be the model of success they could pimp to every would-be drug dealer in Wonderland.

Dealing was a shitty job, complete with terrible hours and low pay. Everybody sees the glamorous side of dealing in the movies, but most dealers make less than minimum wage, and their hazard pay is shit. Criminals needed dealers like the bunny to make it look glamorous.

Eventually, the bunny stopped in front of a club I heard about more than once back on the beat; The Looking Glass Lounge. It was a hotbed of drug activity since before the Red Queen. Girls and boys loved getting all dolled up, snorting Rabbit, and dancing their faces off until it was time to fuck. The Looking Glass Lounge had more ODs than any other club in Wonderland, and why shouldn't it? That's what made it famous.

Thirty years ago, the Looking Glass was home to one of the great ODs in history, the OD that sent the Red Queen's whole world crashing down. Everybody wanted to relive that night, especially those with a fondness for Rabbit.

The Looking Glass had been an institution in Wonderland from the first moment the Red Queen wrested power from her mother. Old Red loved to party, and the Looking Glass was her favorite club. Per eyewitness accounts, before her coronation, the Queen snorted coke with the court jester for three nights straight. During week-long benders as a teenager, she'd disappear into its dark corners with all sorts of men and women. Her ecstatic screams could be heard above even the loudest DJ in the place.

After the coronation, it wasn't proper for the Queen to cavort in such an unseemly place, but she kept the party going in the dungeons and cellars of her castle, with very discreet guests who never revealed her tawdry affairs.

Even without her, the party went on at the Looking Glass club, night after night. People experimented with drugs, their bodies, and even reality itself. It was here that a dealer called The Mad Hatter concocted the first prototypes of White Rabbit and started distributing it to hungry clubbers. News of the drug spread quickly. Partiers raved about it. The Queen, having never met a drug she didn't like, called the Mad Hatter to court.

After tasting White Rabbit, the Queen, in her wisdom, offered the Hatter a job perfecting the drug for mass-market consumption. The Hatter thought it a joke at first. After all, what monarch would want to dabble in drug dealing? But the Queen had a plan. She wanted to turn all of Wonderland into a paradise, replete with wonders the human brain could never imagine in the doldrums of reality.

Her vision was a city consumed with wonder, where every person lived out their every fantasy. This was a message the Hatter could get behind, having devoted his life to madness. He agreed, in secret, to perfect the Queen's formula. He ended up being the key witness in the Queen's trials, turning state's evidence in exchange for immunity.

Once he perfected the formula, the Queen set about her plan, diluting the drugs into the water system so the city would go loopy. She called it "unadulterated madness."

The Looking Glass thrived in the chaos. When foreign dignitaries entered her kingdom, their first stop was the Looking Glass to taste the "Wonderland Way." It was at the Looking Glass that the dignitaries had their first sip of Wonderland's water and fell in love with the madness within its walls.

Every week a parade started at the Queen's palace and ended at the Looking Glass, where she invited all of Wonderland to drink and be merry. And that's exactly what they did. Life wasn't perfect before the fall of the Red Queen, but it was a whole fuck ton merrier.

And that brings us to the night it all came crashing down on the Red Queen. The night of Julemberwary 16, 2613. We've since reverted to the old month structure, but back then, everything was just clusterfucked together in one big gangbang of mashed together weeks.

There was a growing contingent of people unhappy with how the Red Queen ran her empire even before that fateful day. For all the happiness of Wonderland, there were massive infrastructure issues. Imports that never came to port. Exports that never left. The economy was shit. The people didn't work. There wasn't enough food. Citizens were dying at an alarming rate. Still, all the Queen cared about was the happiness of her people, and her people were gleefully, blissfully, and irrevocably happy.

That night was the last night of the summer bash at the Looking Glass. The Mad Hatter had released a stronger, more potent version of White Rabbit and people ate it up, literally. Not only in the water but also in the cakes and cookies the Red Queen served at all her festivals.

We still don't know the exact reason, but at 3:04 a.m., in the middle of the club, people started convulsing and dropping like flies. The music screeched to a halt as the DJ keeled over, dead. The panic set in almost immediately, and the elevated heart rate of the panicked clubbers caused even more hearts to explode.

By the end of the night, 213 partygoers were dead. They hospitalized another 359. The scandal consumed the papers for months. Less than a year later, the council jailed the Red Queen. They purified the water, and people went on with their lives, for better or worse. I always wondered, if those who died could come back to life but be forced to live in the shithole Wonderland has become, would they do it, or would they stay dead?

*What is that stupid bunny doing inside the Looking Glass?* Was he getting more product? Getting his rocks off? Chilling after a long day of dealing death? I couldn't rightly find out. The world outside might have forgotten who I was, but the seedy underbelly of Wonderland would spot me in a heartbeat. If I wanted to take down the bunny, I had to get my job back so I could take him down from the inside. I would have to go back on active duty and rejoin the working world.

My sister had left by the time I walked back to the coffee shop. I often ditched her without saying a word. An hour later, she sent me a text message: *Hope you had a good reason.*

I responded with one word: N*ope.*

I did have a good reason, but I didn't want her to worry. Besides, I was a private person. It might not look it from the massive television exposure, but before I blew up in the media, only three people in the universe knew where I lived: Dormouse, my sister, and the captain. I wasn't much for sharing. I wasn't much for being around humans. I wasn't much for anything except my job, a job I had to earn back.

# CHAPTER EIGHT

The NARCO station was dingier than I remembered before my arrest, but so was all of Wonderland. My station was no different. Its façade hadn't been updated in a hundred years. Gum and tape held the stucco walls together. Still, it looked cool, like the set of an old-timey gangster movie, as long as nobody sneezed and blew it all down.

Sleek, black desks covered every inch of the station. Detectives hunched over their desks, inputting case files into their computers and laughing around the water coolers speckling the precinct. At the back of the station, behind a glass wall, was Aman, the NARCO captain. Round, plump, and bald, Aman stayed on the job past his prime. In his day, he was a formidable Lory bureaucrat before he became a pencil-pushing detective who worked his way up through the system into power. Now, he spent his days wielding that power every chance he got.

Nobody respected him, or the Lory political party for that matter. They hadn't held power since the toppling of the Red Queen. Lories were the dissident party that threw her out of office before they took over running things. They installed the city council to judge the queen and keep order, then created the NARCO division; they're the ones who gave it so much power. However, the Roses broke off from the Lories soon after and wrested control from them. They've kept that power for over two decades, slowly whittling away Lory power into an ineffective shell of itself.

I had no love for Roses, either. I just wanted to do my job, and politics always muddied those waters. There wasn't a drug bust that both parties didn't try to use to their advantage through fear-mongering and xenophobia.

Both parties came down hard on me after the incident. It was an election year, after all, and a redistricting year at that, so they were vehement that I be prosecuted to the fullest extent of the law. Having a killer on the squad was bad for business—bad for votes. Councilmembers from both sides picketed outside my door, crafting stump speeches that even made *me* hate me more. Politicians knew how to build a lather.

And leave it to them to move on the moment public interest waned, which is exactly what happened once people stopped protesting outside my apartment in force. I'm sure they have another picket line to rile up across town protesting some other bullshit thing—anything for a vote.

"Get your ass in here, Liddell," Aman screamed from his office, seated on his fat ass, the moment he noticed me. Why would he bother standing up and walking outside? I trudged into his cramped office, which smelled of old man sweat and ass crack.

"Yes, Captain?" I said sheepishly.

"It's good to see you, kid. It's real good to see you. Have a seat."

I didn't want to sit on the half-eaten pizza in a greasy box currently occupying the seat. "I've been sittin' on my ass for a long while, sir. I'm ready to get back to it."

Aman cleared his throat. "You sure about that, Liddell? I know how hard this can be for a detective."

"I'm ready, sir. I can't sit and eat one more bonbon or listen to one more bullshit daytime soap. Not while that fucking bunny is still on the street."

Aman nodded solemnly. "Well, you know I can't just put you back on active duty, kid." The word "kid" grated on my nerves. "You've been through a trauma. Department procedure says you gotta be on desk duty 'til a shrink clears you, and you pass a gun test."

"Fuck procedure, Captain. I'm ready!"

He chuckled. "I got no doubt of that, kiddo, but rules are rules. My hands are tied. I'll get the shrink to call you. Meanwhile, enjoy your vacation."

"Just make the appointment. I need to get back out there."

I bumped into Dormouse on the way out the door, but I had no intention of stopping. "Where the hell are you going?" he shouted as I raced through the door, but I couldn't let him see me break. I couldn't let him see me cry.

You couldn't cry in the NARCO squad. Hell, you couldn't cry anywhere in Wonderland. You had to be hard as steel. I never broke, not for any reason, until the moment I woke up in that hospital.

I thought I was forged in the fire, but after the crucible I just ran, Aman's dismissal cracked me. I needed a win. I needed something to go right. I finally had wind in my sails. I finally had a purpose. And it was taken away from me in an instant. No. Fuck that. I wasn't going to let that happen. I wouldn't let them take the first good thing that happened in the last few months away from me. If they weren't going to let me back on the force, I'd catch that fucking bunny myself.

They scheduled an appointment for me at the headshrinker the next day. Either I was an urgently tragic case, or he was a particularly horrendous doctor. I've never gotten in to see a doctor so quickly in all my life.

"I'm going to ask you a series of questions," he said. "And all you have to do is answer them honestly. Are you ready?"

"No."

"Excuse me?"

"You want me to be honest, right? And I'm not ready. I'm not ready for any of this."

The doctor wore glasses, and his hair parted down the middle. The tips of his hair were frayed and flipped up, and his bangs fell into his face every few minutes. He used thick gel to hold it in place, but it still flopped down over and over again. If I were him, I would have shaved it all off. I liked guys with bald heads. They looked like walruses. My dad used to think he was a walrus. I wonder what he would think now, his daughter as crazy as him. Would he get a kick out of it because I was a chip off the old block, or would he be ashamed of me for falling into his pattern of psychoses?

"I think there is another way," the doctor said. "I won't ask you any questions. Just tell me about your day. Spare no detail."

"This must be boring for you, hearing about people's mundane lives."

He chuckled. "Sometimes, but you would be surprised how much you can reveal if you listen to somebody blather on."

He was right. I already knew he hated his job. He fidgeted in his chair, which meant he lacked confidence. He looked away from my eyes when he spoke to me because he feared I would catch on to his bullshit. He was a lying pussy, whose only power lay in the degrees lining his walls.

"Today was particularly tedious. I got up, got out of bed, and ran a comb across my head. Then, I grabbed my coat and my hat—"

"Let me guess. You made the bus in seconds flat."

"This is my story. Quit interrupting, and no. I walked."

"See, I already know two things about you. You are funny, and you like the Beatles."

"Who doesn't like the Beatles?"

"You would be surprised."

I sat up in my chair. "Nothing surprises me."

The rest of the session went reasonably well. We talked about the Beatles and how Ringo Starr was the best narrator of all time. We talked about *Sergeant Pepper* and *Help!* and, well, those were the only albums we could remember. I had trouble with my memory since taking Rabbit. Eventually, the buzzer rang, and it was time to leave.

"This has been a good first session, Alice. I hope to see you back next week."

I stood. "Hey, Doc. How many sessions until I fix this shit and get back to work?"

"As many as you need."

"And how many is that? Three? Five? Forty?"

He smiled again. "Trust the process. Meanwhile, practice your marksmanship. You'll need it soon enough."

"Thanks, Doctor."

Like I needed marksmanship training. I could shoot the apple off a crow's head at half a mile even if I were drunk. I wasn't going to the shooting range, but I wasn't resting on my laurels either. I was going to take down the bunny, whether I had the department's support or not.

# CHAPTER NINE

There is nothing more boring than a stakeout. It's all the fun of a standardized test mixed with the excitement of a ten-hour opera. Usually, I had a partner on my stakeouts, but I couldn't ask Dormouse to risk his career to bring down the bunny with me.

I hadn't been in front of the Looking Glass Club long, but one thing was abundantly clear already: they did not fuck around with security. Three patrols walked between the front and back of the club in shifts. They staggered their patrols and never left one guard unit patrolling for more than an hour at a time. On the roof of the Looking Glass and every building around it, snipers and lookouts were armed and ready to kill anyone dumb enough to walk up unannounced.

Clubbers needed a special card to prove they were members. There were some rich-ass bitches and fuckbois that went into this place; a who's who of the cultural elite. The children of mayors, councilors, and every famous person in Wonderland strolled through their doors.

Some rumors say the Queen never gave up control of the Looking Glass. Others say the city councilors never wanted to help Wonderland. They just wanted the Looking Glass for their own.

I tend to think the explanation is simpler. The Queen went to jail, all her cronies went to jail, and that left a power vacuum in the city that some new scumbag filled without missing a beat. I'm not big on conspiracy theories. I've been doing this a long time, and it's always the easiest, simplest explanations that end up being the truth.

There's never a big web of lies, and it was always easy to connect point A to point B once you knew which thread to pull. Hell, usually, we knew who was guilty within ten minutes of taking a case, and we spent all our time proving it.

Just then, there was a knock on the window, the gentle rapping of a gun. Metal on glass made an undeniable sound. A head lowered down to the driver's side window and grinned at me. A puff of smoke came out of its mouth. As the smoke cleared, I saw that his hairless body changed colors with the nodes. Green nodes lined his bald head on either side. Then they were pink…then orange.

"Please roll down your whindow," the man said with a wispy lisp.

In my rearview mirror, two goons stood stoically, complementing the ones at my driver's side and passenger doors. There was no escape, so I complied.

"And whoo arrrre yoou?" He blew a thick cloud of smoke into my face.

I didn't cough. I couldn't show weakness. Even in the face of incredible odds, I had to be brave. "My name—"

"Dooon't lie, my dear. I whill know if you are lying, and I detest liars."

"Then I'm at an impasse. If I lie, you will shoot me, and if I tell the truth, you'll shoot me."

The man chuckled. "Whell played, Ms. Liddell. Whell played."

"It's Detective Liddell, and how did you know my name?"

"I don't think it is 'detective'. Not anymore. As I heard it, yhou are on suspension, which makes the fhact yhou are outside of my club even more mysterious."

"My car broke down."

"Again, please do not lie. I do know everything, yhou see."

I sighed. "I'm looking for somebody."

"Whell, I know many people. What does this person look like?"

"Like a giant bunny."

The man opened the door for me. "Hmm…yes, yes. I know the chap. Come inside with me, and let's see if I can help yhou right offh."

I stepped out of the car. "No offense, but if you are going to kill me, I'd rather it be outside."

He grinned slyly. "Kill yhou? I'm not going to kill yhou. That's sooooo gauche. I'm going to help yhou."

"Why would you help me?"

He leaned in toward me. "Because whee can't have nastiness whalking the streets now, can we? That whould be bedlam. I promise yhou, on my whord as a businessman and the health of my dearest possessions, my men will not harm yhou."

I cautiously followed behind the man, his legs inching forward in tandem as his hips swayed side to side. Watching his walk, I finally placed him. He was the Caterpillar.

The Caterpillar had been an opium den proprietor for decades before the fall of the Red Queen. He made good buying legitimate businesses after she was arrested. Once her biggest competitor, he gained the most from her downfall. Of course, the files never said he owned the Looking Glass. Up until now, nobody knew who owned it. I must've been the first one.

# CHAPTER TEN

"I don't whant yhou to be nervhous," Caterpillar said after we sat down in his private box overlooking the club. "After all, I am a businessman, and shooting a NARCO, no matter how unlikeable she is, whould be bad…fhor business."

I could barely hear him through the thumping noise in the club. I recognized every famous face on the dance floor, shaking their asses and grinding against their soon-to-be lovers.

"Complete debauchery, right?" the Caterpillar said with a grin.

"Complete. I can't believe that I'm the first NARCO seeing it."

He chuckled. "Oh honey, you really are naïve. Look there."

Caterpillar pointed to the back of the club, where a coquettish waitress was grinding hard against a plump Aman. *My NARCO captain.*

"Yhou can't really believe I could get where I am whithout some powerfhul fhriends, could yhou?"

A waitress placed two water glasses in front of us. "Then what do you need with me?"

Caterpillar pushed the glass over to me. "Yhou will be my greatest redemption story. The bad NARCO made good. And in return, yhou whill be very appreciative. Drink up."

The Caterpillar swigged down his glass. "Unfhortunately, this whater does nothing for me, but it should give yhou quite the buzz. It might even send yhou into another whorld."

I pushed the glass away. "I've seen what Rabbit does, and I'm not interested."

*I was lying.*

He grinned for a moment, then leaned back in his lounge chair, taking a deep puff of his pipe.

"That is yhour right. Just know my fhriends tend to get fhavors affhorded them. I am less generous with people who are impolite."

I stood. "I don't need your favors."

"Oh, don't yhou? Do yhou think the NARCOs whill let yhou back on the streets unless I tell them it's a good idea? Do yhou really think they whant to let an offhicer who shoots children back onto the fhorce?"

"I'll take my chances."

"So be it, but yhou'll never fhind the bunny whithout my help, and yhou'll never get back on the fhorce whithout the bunny behind bars."

"Like I said, I'll take my chances."

"Fhair enough, but don't yhou whant to hear my offher, even a little bit? I'm very reasonable. Look at yhour captain. Doesn't he look like he's having fhun?"

I sighed. Deep down in my bones, I did want to hear his offer. I couldn't help myself. Any chance to get back on the force without sitting through more head shrinking was worth the risk.

"What is it?"

"All yhou have to do is take a drink of that whater. In exchange, I hand-deliver the bunny to you. Yhou become the big hero. Yhou return to the fhorce. Yhou get everything you ever whanted."

"And then I'm in your pocket forever."

"Fhriends don't have pockets. All I whant is fhor us to be fhriends. Yhou could use a fhriend right now, couldn't yhou? Yhour sister whon't alwhays be there." He tapped the glass over to me. "Just one drink, and it whill all be over."

I wanted to move. I tried to pull my feet toward the door, but they resisted me. "What have you done with the bunny?"

"He's in a safhe place. Held up until yhou make your decision. If yhou agree, huzzah, the bunny is yhours. If not, he gets thrown in a lake, and yhou'll never get back on the squad."

"At least he'll be off the streets."

"But so whill yhou. Can yhou live with yhourself if that happened? Can yhou live a lifhe as an offhice drone, or a private investigator, scrounging fhor scraps? Do yhou really hate power so much yhou'll let it fhall through your fhingers?"

I picked up the glass. "How do I know you aren't manipulating me?"

"Everything is manipulation, my dear Alice. At least I'm honest about it." He sat forward. "Now to the truth of it. Yhou have two options. Yhou can drink and be merry, or yhou can whalk out. If yhou whalk out, yhou will never, ever, be a detective again. Yhou whill never fhix this blemish on yhour record. Yhou whill be a pariah for the rest of your lifhe. The media may die down, but every job application whill come with a rejection. Nobody whill hire a child killer. Yhou must change yhour name, move, and start over. Maybe with yhour sister—Dinah, is it?—in that nice one-horse town she lives in with her fhamily."

"Is that a threat?"

He chuckled. "Not unless yhou take it as one. Not unless that lifhe doesn't appeal to yhou. If it does, go and live in the doldrums. But if yhou whant your old lifhe back, then now is the time to act. Sip and be merry or live in eternal shame."

I wanted to leave, but I couldn't. The glass touched my lips almost against my will. I tilted it back and finished the cup in one swig. "Now what? How long until it takes effect?"

"Oh, there was no Rabbit in that glass, my dear. That was more symbolic than anything. I can't have yhou zonked out on Rabbit. Not now. Yhou have whork to do now. Yhou're going to be a star."

Caterpillar snapped his fingers, and two burly men dragged a beaten bunny into the room. It was the first time I got a good look at his face. Gone were the perfectly manicured whiskers and soft fur. All that remained were bloody holes and matted, sweaty hair.

I wanted to pull out my gun to shoot him dead, but I didn't sell my soul for nothing. I sold it to make everything right again. I sighed under my breath. There was no turning back now.

# CHAPTER ELEVEN

The bunny squirmed as I struggled to push him through the front door of the police station.  Caterpillar must have tipped off every media outlet in the city because a horde of photographers snapped photos as I moved through them as reporters screamed questions at me. I still didn't like crowds, but it was a far cry better than being pelted with rotten fruit and yelled at to die.

Aman met me at the front of the precinct with three uniformed officers. His lips were pursed and turned up in a snarl. Gone was the pleasant tone he held with me during our last meeting. Now, he was gruff and bitter. "I thought I told you to stay out of field work."

I shrugged, gripping the scruff of the bunny's neck tighter until he let out a pained yelp. "I was out getting a froyo, and I saw this one dealing to a couple of kids. What was I supposed to do? Let him go?"

"Yes!" Aman screamed, flailing his doughy arms into the air. "Let the NARCOs who can pass their firing range test deal with it. You're on desk duty."

I stepped forward, pushing the bunny to the uniforms next to Aman. "I couldn't do that. Consider it a citizen's arrest if nothing else." I stared deep into his eyes. "We can all use a win, Captain, and if nothing else, 'bad cop makes good' is good publicity."

He growled loudly under his breath. "You're not making this easy for me."

My eyes narrowed. "I'm not trying to make it easy. I'm trying to do my job. Now, are you going to scold me more, or can I write up this report?"

"I don't like this," Aman looked past me to the reporters crowding against the door like a pack of mindless zombies. "But I guess you earned your way off desk duty, if for no other reason than if I kept you grounded, it would be all over the media. You make one false move, though, and I'll bust you down so fast you'll beg to scrub toilets. Got it?"

I smiled. "Absolutely, Captain. You won't regret this."

He turned back to the elevator. "I already do."

My perp-walking the bunny into the jail made front-page news. Radio jockeys argued whether I should be locked up with him, but at least they weren't making lewd comments about my breasts anymore. The public returned to protest outside my window, but this time those who wanted me run out of town were met with a counterprotest demanding I be given a second chance. I hated them both, but it was a far cry better than the whole city demanding my head on a pike.

Still, I would have rather they left me alone. After all, it was hard to do my job when the whole city knew my name. Detectives were supposed to be incognito, below the radar, and making the front page of the paper made me a minor celebrity. Every criminal in the city would know my face by the end of the week.

I found it hard to worry about that kind of thing, though, as I cradled my badge tightly in my hand. No, as I clipped it to my belt, all I felt was pride, and victory, after so much defeat—after so much regret.

The only problem was that the badge came with a cost. I was now indebted to the Caterpillar, and I had no idea what that meant. I was a good cop, or at least I had been a good cop. I followed the rules and kept my nose clean, even though half my department was on the take. Half was probably being generous since Dormouse was the only one I knew for sure was clean. Nobody talked about it out in the open, of course, but most of the NARCOs wore watches too nice for their salary and drove cars out of the price range of any public servant.

Caterpillar wasn't my first offer, either. Every criminal in the city wanted a NARCO in their pocket to wipe the slate clean for them in a pinch. It made the job a hundred times harder because you had to fight the rot outside the precinct and the rot festering inside it. More than a few of my perps got off because a stash of drugs, or a weapon they used to kill their rivals, went missing in the days before a trial.

Nobody said much about it because the problem was endemic, and nobody wanted to blow up their spot. All we could do were our jobs and try to bust as many bad guys as possible. Those who weren't on the take used subterfuge, safe houses, and other tricks to keep the corrupt narcs from destroying everything we worked for, and now I was part of the rot.

I was a good get, too, because I had always been outspoken about my hatred for dirty narcs. It would have gotten me in trouble if Dormouse didn't back me up. Somehow, even though he hated the rotten ones as much as me, they liked him well enough. Maybe it was because he did their paperwork after a bust or because he brought in doughnuts every week, but whatever the reason, they accepted him while keeping me at arm's distance.

I had my suspicions that, because he was a man, even a black man, it put them at ease more than seeing me, a woman with what they deemed was a "nasty personality," working alongside them and even outshining them on my best days. They all must have reveled when I fell from my perch as the golden child into the muck with them. I even saw a dart board along the wall that had a picture of my mugshot from when I made the front page of the paper, with a half dozen darts stuck through my head and neck.

"Hey, dyke!" a tall, bearded lieutenant shouted as I walked through the precinct to my desk, as if there was something wrong with being a lesbian. His name was Deacon, and I hated him. "I thought we were finally rid of you."

"Well," I snorted, "I guess you're stuck with me a bit longer."

"What did you have to do to get off desk duty?" his partner, Collins, chuckled out at me. "Suck off the captain?"

I spun to him as he reached out to grab my arm. "No, I had to do my job better than you, just like every other day."

Deacon leaned forward. "Does that include killing little children?"

"I'll—" I lunged at him, but I fell into Dormouse's big, muscular hands as they pulled me away from a confrontation.

"Don't give them the satisfaction," he whispered. "They're looking for any reason to get you kicked out, and if you give them one, they win."

He was right, and I knew he was right. I stood straight and brushed myself off. I had a badge, and that's all I ever wanted. I wasn't about to ruin that again.

"Next time, your partner won't be around to protect you," Collins said, rolling his tongue over his lips.

"Don't get it twisted," Dormouse said. "I was saving you from her, not the other way around."

"Thanks," I said, walking toward the back of the bullpen.

"You're being an idiot," Dormouse said, grabbing a manila folder. "And I won't always be there to save you from yourself."

"You already weren't." I bit my lip after the words slipped out. "Sorry."

He wasn't there the night I shot—the night I failed to take down the bunny and ended up in traction. He was supposed to be stationed up in the alley to stop the bunny from escaping, posing as a homeless drunk, but he called out sick. I often thought about what would have happened if he had been there that night, but it wasn't his fault, no matter how much my fucked-up mind tried to convince me otherwise.

"Come on," he said, avoiding my words. "We have a case."

# CHAPTER TWELVE

"Are you serious?" I said, staring through the broken glass into a ransacked burger shop. It was a standard B&E, with a little vandalism thrown in for good measure. I hadn't worked something so banal since my early days out of the academy. "This is beneath me."

Dormouse shook his head. "That's the problem with you, Liddell. You think everything is beneath you unless it's some big case, and even then, if you're not the lead, you're not interested." He stepped over the broken glass into the shop. "That's why everybody hates you. It's not because you're a woman. It's because you are a prick."

I sighed and opened the door next to the broken window. Somebody spray-painted a red rabbit over a layer of white paint. The smiling rabbit giving a thumbs-up was the symbol of White Rabbit during the Red Queen's reign.

"You're a prick, and people still like you. It's a double standard. People like you because you're a prick with a prick, and they hate me because I'm a prick without one."

Dormouse rolled his eyes. "Just go find the owner. The uniform officers have him next door, but you know they'll only get half the story."

"Interview duty? You're seriously trying to pawn interview duty off on me? Didn't you just tell me you were the one people liked?" I threw my hands in the air. "Why are we even here? This is a simple B&E. Nobody got hurt. Why can't the uniforms handle it?"

Dormouse pointed to a mural on the wall—another red rabbit, this time drawn on half the wall instead of just the door. "Captain thinks somebody is sending a message, and we need to figure out who it is before they strike again."

I scratched my head. "It's a bunch of dumb teenagers the owner probably pissed off. Case closed."

Dormouse walked toward me. "You were so anxious to get off desk duty, and now you're complaining about being out in the field. There's no way to win with you, is there? You just want to complain."

I growled at him. "Fine, I will go interview the shop owner. Twenty bucks says he knows who destroyed his shop and he's just not saying."

Dormouse smiled, and his bright white teeth lit up half the room. "You're really good about convincing people to tell you what you want to know."

I turned to the door. "Because I'm so annoying, right?"

"Something like that," he replied.

I stepped out of the creaky door. When it had been closed, I didn't notice it barely hung on its hinges, but now it swung low, nearly clipping the top of my head as I passed. I stood outside the door for a long moment, catching the mid-morning sun on my face. The air tinged with urine, as it always did in Crash Town.

It was the neighborhood I grew up in, full of junkies and tweakers strung out on Rabbit. Break-ins were nothing unusual, and all the businesses had gates that closed tight at night, which begged the question, what happened to this poor shmuck's lock that allowed people to vandalize it?

I stepped over shattered glass all over the ground, and something hit me. If the hooligans who roughed up the place smashed through the front window, then the glass would have shattered inward, not outward. I walked back up to the door and ran my hand down the front of it. Sure enough, there was no paint on it. They painted the inside to make it look like it was done on the outside.

It didn't make much sense, but then nothing did these days. I decided to file it in the back of my mind and speak with the store owner. I headed next door to a small bodega and found a petite woman with long wrinkles grooved into her face, surrounded by a small squadron of uniforms.

"I'll take it from here, boys," I said, walking toward them. I ran into the pair before, and they were begrudgingly ambivalent to my existence, which was a blessing given the past few weeks.

The officers grunted to each other, shook their heads, and took their leaves. The woman stood to do the same, but I held up my hand to her. "I'm afraid I need you to stay put, miss. I have a couple of questions for you."

She shook her head. "I already answered everything. I have to clean up my shop."

"Ma'am, I'm afraid that's not possible. It's an active crime scene until we're done with our investigation. Now, can you please repeat what you told the officers?"

She crossed her arms in a huff. "I don't know much. I came in this morning, and everything was a mess. Chairs were flipped over. The walls were graffitied, and the till was empty. Those kids are stupid, though, because I emptied it overnight. I don't trust anyone, and now I know why."

"Is there anyone you can think of who would want to hurt you?"

"Of course!" she shouted. "I'm the only business on the block that doesn't kowtow to the Cards."

The Cards were the biggest gang in Wonderland. They used to be the Red Queen's personal thugs, but when she was arrested, they went rogue and started working on their own dealing drugs, running guns, laundering money, and offering protection.

"Did you give a key to anyone?" I asked, flipping open a notepad. "It seems like the vandalism started inside and then moved outside."

She rolled her tongue around in her mouth. "That would make sense. I kept a key for the door under the register just in case."

"And who would have access to it?"

She shook her head. "I don't give the key to anyone. Just myself, and my—" She placed her hand on her mouth. "No, no, no. It's not possible."

"Who?" I asked. "If you know something, you need to tell me."

"My nephew," she said, clenching her fists, trying to hide her anger. "He swore to me he would not join them."

"I am going to need the name of your nephew. And an address."

"His name is Yin. And he doesn't live far."

# CHAPTER THIRTEEN

Yin's apartment wasn't far from the shop. Nothing was far in Wonderland. The slums of Crash Town were only a few blocks from Antieque, a luxury fashion mall, and a chic neighborhood with brownstones worth ten times more than the apartments where I grew up. Nobody knew how they decided which areas were expensive and which were cheap, but it always seemed arbitrary to me.

"Be ready for him to flee," Dormouse said as we walked up the half-condemned building to the third floor. The fire escape was the easiest method of escape if Yin decided to run, and we asked the uniforms to guard the bottom just in case. They didn't like plain-clothes officers much, but there wasn't much they could do about it either. There was a hierarchy, which made my descent into the muck all the sweeter for them.

I knocked lightly on the door and then turned from it just in case they were armed inside and wanted to take potshots at the door.

"Mrs. Ling. We're looking for Yin. Can you please open the door?"

Footsteps casually shuffled to the door and opened it. The woman on the other end had been crying recently. Her face was puffy and red, and her eyes bloodshot. I had seen the same face a hundred times in my career and looked at it in the mirror most every morning while I was on sabbatical.

"Mrs. Ling," Dormouse said. "Is Yin here? His aunt said—"

"No," Mrs. Ling replied. "He didn't come home last night. I haven't seen him in two days. Why, what happened?"

"I'm afraid your son is a suspect in a break-in at his aunt's restaurant."

Mrs. Ling shook her head vigorously. "No, that's not possible. He loved that store. He talked about taking it over after he was done with school all the time."

"Things change, Mrs. Ling," Dormouse said. "But I hope that this was all a misunderstanding. Do you have any idea where he would hang out? Did he talk to you about any friends he might be hanging out with?"

She shook her head again. "No, nothing like that. He was focused on schoolwork and graduating. He didn't have time for friends or anything else."

It was a tale as old as time. Yin was hiding something, maybe everything, from his mother, and meanwhile, she thought he was the perfect son. Teenagers were the worst that way. I saw it dozens of times.

"Do you mind if we come in and look through your son's room? It might give us a hint about where he is."

She hesitated. "I don't know. They say I shouldn't let you in without a warrant."

"I understand," Dormouse said. "But to get a warrant, we'll have to go to city hall, which means precious minutes if your son is really gone. It would help both of us if you let us in to do our job and, if you're right, then prove your son's innocence."

"I—" Her eyes shifted back and forth before she pursed her lips. "I think you will need to get a warrant."

I sighed. "You're making a mistake, Mrs. Ling."

"Maybe," she replied. "But it's mine to make, Detective Liddell."

"How—" I hadn't told the woman my name, but then I realized that she must have seen me on the news, which would have explained the daggers she dug into my chest with her eyes. "I'm not going to hurt your son. I'm trying to help him."

"You keep telling yourself that," she said. "But I have seen what you do to children, so forgive me if I don't believe you."

She shut the door on me and slammed it in my face before I could defend myself. I went to knock on the door again, but Dormouse stopped me, shaking his head as he lowered my hand to the ground.

"It's not worth it."

"I'm not like that," I replied, tears welling in my eyes.

He pulled a tissue out of his pocket and handed it to me. "I know."

I dabbed the tissue on my eyes as I turned from him. "I thought, bringing in the bunny—I thought that would make everything okay, again, but I guess it will never be okay, all the way, will it?"

"We all have our burdens, Alice." He turned me around. "Look at me. I'm a big, strong, black man who chose to be a NARCO. How do you think people look at me when I go back to my own block?"

I shrugged. "I assumed everyone loved you everywhere."

He chuckled. "Far from it, and the things I have heard when I arrest somebody. Woof. Do you remember what that tweaker called me when we pulled him out of that dumpster?"

I nodded. I did, and it was not pleasant; certainly not something to be repeated even in the most intimate company. "I'm sorry."

He shrugged. "It's part of the job. If you believe in the job and what we're doing, you have to accept that people are going to hate you. Now they have one more reason."

I sighed. "This is a hell of a pep talk."

"I'm not trying to talk you up. I'm trying to give you some reality. Now, quit crying because we have work to do. The last thing I need is a hysterical partner weighing me down."

I wiped the rest of the tears from my eyes. "I'm good. I'm good."

He turned to the stairs. "It's okay if you're not, but you shouldn't be in the field if you're not. If you're here, then you have to be here fully. Got it?"

I nodded. "You're right. I got it."

"Then let's hop to it."

# CHAPTER FOURTEEN

I hated City Hall. I found myself at the courthouse more days than I cared to admit, testifying on cases, or appearing in front of grand juries, and the nauseous feeling I got after passing under the archway into the marble-floored expanse of the building never got any better. When the Red Queen ruled, City Hall acted as her main palace, where she would entertain guests, and when the Lories overwhelmed her, they converted it into the monstrosity it became in her wake.

Despite the fact that the Lories had not been in power for many decades, every doorway had little birds carved into it, and the walls were wallpapered with them everywhere. Black and white checkered marble tiles lined the main hallway, where hundreds of men and women in power suits clomped along, echoing through the room.

A huge oak information desk stood in the center of the room, with a uniformed NARCO officer swiveling around it. I didn't like uniformed officers, but even I had to admit that desk duty in City Hall was beneath even them. However, the NARCOs were the Roses' personal police force and had been since they took power from the Tories. Though they started with simply busting White Rabbit and various drug crimes, soon their budget overwhelmed the police department, and our jobs expanded to everything from murder to armed robbery.

The desk officer recognized both of us, and instead of having to sign in, we were waved through down the endless corridors of the building. I often wondered which rooms were where the Red Queen had orgies and entertained diplomats with her special brand of drug-induced stupors, but the Roses played that close to their chests. After all, how much authority would one have if a criminal found out their courtroom was orgy central?

"Can you file the warrant?" Dormouse asked. "I have to check with Charlotte about something."

Charlotte was Dormouse's wife and a court reporter; one of the best, it turned out. Her fastidious attention to detail dwarfed even her husband's, which made it impossible to get one past her, a quality I very much respected.

"It's fine. Go find your wife."

The courthouse took up most of City Hall, but there were plenty of offices for the city council and other government departments. You could find just about anything related to the city inside its walls or in the buildings surrounding it, which were considerably less auspicious than the palace.

I followed the hallways until they dead-ended at a flight of wooden stairs that led both up into the offices and down into the bowels of the building. I took the stairs down toward the basement into the records room, where a kindly old man with thick glasses oversaw all the paperwork for the court.

"Morning, Mateo," I said with a wave. He didn't respond or even look up from his papers. The room was a maze of different filings, and only Mateo knew how they all fit together. I often thought that he kept it messy so he couldn't be fired because nobody, even Dormouse's wife, could put everything back in order again.

The petition for a warrant was long and tedious. It took over half an hour to fill it out, and in the middle of it, I realized that Dormouse probably said he had to find his wife to get out of the tedious work that undergirded all police work. I liked to do the fun, fast work of being a

NARCO officer, but most of it was the slow, plodding work of crossing your t's and dotting your i's.

When I was done, I placed the warrant on the pile and left it for Mateo. He would buzz me when the judge was ready to hear my petition, which could take an hour or a couple of days. Meanwhile, I could track down a couple of more leads and try to find Yin my own way by keeping my boots on the ground. I hoped I wouldn't even need the stupid warrant in the end, and if I did my job right, I wouldn't. There were plenty of neighbors to ask and friends at school, which could help me triangulate Yin's location if his mother wouldn't help me. All I needed was one to open up to me.

I took the stairs back up to the main floor two at a time, and when I turned to the door, I ran straight into a tall woman with a tight bun, crashing into her so hard that I sent her papers flying into the air.

"Oh shit!" I shouted. "I'm so sorry."

I grabbed as many papers as I could out of the air as the woman dropped to the ground to gather them up. "It's quite all right, Officer Liddell. I wasn't paying attention to where I was going."

I finished grabbing the papers and handed them to her. "How do you know my name?"

"It's my job to know everything that goes on in this town. I assume you don't know me, then." I shook my head as she stood up. "Councilwoman Lane."

She held out her hand, and I shook it. My case reached the Council, so of course, she knew me. "Sorry, of course. I was just flustered."

Councilwoman Lane led the Roses to a historic victory fifteen years ago. The Lories slowly gained ground over the past several elections, but the councilwoman was able to use the arrest of a high-value White Rabbit dealer on the Lories's territory to turn the tides and take over a supermajority of the council. She loved getting her picture taken, too, so she was everywhere.

"It's quite all right." She smiled. "It's not very often somebody can pull the spotlight from me, so I tend to take notice when they do, and you have managed to do it twice in one month."

"I'm sorry about that," I said. "Trust me; it's the last thing I wanted. I just want to be a cog in a machine, ma'am, not somebody who's in the spotlight."

"Well, that makes this very awkward, then," she said with a smile.

"What does?"

"Well, I intended to have my people call you to set this up, but I thought after your last heroic deed, it would be a good idea to present you with a medal to recognize your rehabilitation and how quickly you sprung back from being knocked down."

I stood straight. "I don't know about that. I'm just trying to do my bit."

She waved me off. "Nonsense. 'Disgraced cop makes good' is great publicity. Don't you want people to think you are a hero again?"

"I—" I nodded. "Yes, I do."

She smiled. "Great. Then I think we can do a ceremony tomorrow morning." She looked down at her watch. "Oh, that's cutting it close, but I'll have my people call your people."

"I don't really have people." But she didn't listen. She was off down the steps, flipping open her phone to place a call. *What the hell just happened?*

# CHAPTER FIFTEEN

Dinah absolutely loved that I had to look nice for the presentation of my medal. Even though it was late by the time I called her, she dropped everything and rushed to my side the next morning with a case full of makeup and hair products.

"You realize I will be wearing a uniform, right?" I asked as she teased and styled my hair.

"And it's going to look hideous because you always look hideous in it, so the least you can do is spruce yourself up for the camera."

I looked at myself in the mirror. My cheeks were red, and my eyes were a deep purple. "I look like a tart. People are going to laugh at me."

"People are already laughing," she said. "When they see you in the paper tomorrow, they'll think, 'Is that Alice Liddell? She doesn't look dead,' and that will be worth it. Maybe you'll even land a man from it." She laughed moments after the words came from her mouth. "Sorry, that was a joke. Even I'm not that much of a miracle worker."

"Just tone it down, okay?" I asked, licking my hand to wash some of the rouge off my cheek. "I don't want to look like a clown."

"You're no fun," she said, but she acquiesced to my demands. By the time she was done, my hair had been pulled into a tight bun, which fit perfectly under my cap. My face looked like it had color, but not too much, and she had even softened the color of my eyes, making them pop as they looked natural.

I stood in front of the mirror when it was all done, dressed in my formal dress uniform, black from head to toe, with only the silver buttons of my shirt and the bars on my cap to break it up.

"Seriously," Dinah said. "This ensemble ruins all my work."

I smiled. "I think it looks nice. Are you going to come today?"

"Of course," she said. "People are finally recognizing that my sister is the best cop around, and I'm gonna be there to honor it."

We loaded into her car and made our way out of the parking lot. The protesters had subdued once again, as had the counter-protesters who took my side. I thought maybe my brush with celebrity was over for a second time, and I could get back to life after this ceremony. However, when we reached the City Hall building, I was bombarded with ten times more protesters than I had ever seen before, half of which marched and chanted horrible things against me, and the other half stood up for me.

"This is weird," Dinah said, pulling through them into the parking structure.

"That's an understatement," I said with a fake smile. "Welcome to my life."

"How do you work like this?"

"It's hard, but I manage, kind of." I sighed. "It's been more harm than good, though, if I am honest with myself."

"Maybe you should move." It was a refrain she often gave. "I know the Sedonus sheriff is looking for a few good men—er, woman."

I laughed. "I'm not up for traffic stops. I like my life here, even if it's hard. This is where I grew up. It's where Mom—it's home to me."

She pulled into a space and put the car in park. "I thought home was where your family was."

"Maybe for you," I replied. "Now, let's get this over with."

Dinah followed my lead up the steps to the main atrium. Reporters lined the hall, and my eyes went wide as they peppered me with questions. Before I could open my mouth, I felt soft hands on my shoulder and allowed a brightly dressed woman to pull me up the stairs. She had huge, multicolored hair, like a peacock, but she had no augmentations to her body.

"There will be time for questions later," she said as we disappeared behind a pillar. When we were alone, she turned to me. "Thank the gods you are here."

"Who are you?" I asked, confused. "I'm not going to my death or anything by following you, am I?"

"Poppy, Councilwoman Lane's press secretary. It's nice to meet you."

"I suppose I can say the same to you, although I wish it were under different circumstances."

She smiled. "Under different circumstances, we would have no reason to."

"It's crazy out there," Dinah said, scampering to keep up with us.

She dropped her horn-rimmed glasses to look at her. "And who are you?"

"That's my sister," I piped up. "She's cool."

She turned back forward. "Not my problem. Keep up if you want to follow us. Now, as for you, Detective Liddell. You will present yourself to the councilwoman and stand behind her as she gives a speech." *Of course, this was a press junket for her—anything for good publicity.* "Then, she will pin a medal on you for bravery or some such garbage. You will get your picture taken, answer questions, and leave. The whole thing should take twenty minutes." She turned to me. "Do you have any problem speaking in public?"

"I mean, I had to do it at my trial, and it was okay," I replied.

"No, that won't do." She shook his head. "Don't talk about your trial here. This isn't about the past but the future. It's hard enough to massage over your image with—"

I stopped. "Why is she trying to massage my image anyway?"

She shrugged. "I don't know, but you must have powerful friends if the councilwoman took a special interest in you. She only bends for power or celebrity."

*Caterpillar.* I had a feeling this was his doing, even if I wanted to believe this was due to my own value, but now it made sense. He wanted a rehabilitated cop on his payroll, and what better way to rehabilitate somebody than to have a medal pinned on them by the City Council?

We finally reached a pair of double-wide doors, and she turned to me, looking me up and down. "You look…fine."

"Thank you," I replied suspiciously. "It was all my sister's doing."

"Hrm," she said, dour. "Well, it will have to do. When the trumpets play, the doors will open, and you walk inside. Got it?"

I nodded. "Got it."

She spun on her heels and walked off. "Don't mess it up."

# CHAPTER SIXTEEN

Butterflies filled my stomach and tickled my throat, making me want to vomit as I waited for the doors to open to my award ceremony. "I have a bad feeling about this."

Dinah rubbed my back. "It's going to be fine. You put one foot in front of the other, breathe. It's going to be great. I'm going to go inside before I ruin everything."

Dinah slid through the door and closed it behind her, leaving me in the hall alone. People mulled, and their hushed voices echoed off the walls. I closed my eyes and tried to center myself, swaying back and forth until the trumpets began to blare.

*Just put one foot in front of the other.*

The doors in front of me opened, and two uniformed officers glowered at me grimly. The floor of the small room was covered with a thin red carpet, with wood panels surrounding it. Gold trimmed chairs filled the room, and other officers sat in most of them, with some members of the public, and my sister, speckling the black-dressed crowd. The flag of Wonderland, a dodo bird, surrounded by a laurel of roses against a white background, hung on either side of the platform at the front of the room. It was the one piece of iconography that survived the Lory Coup. Councilwoman Lane stood behind a wooden podium with a professional smile on her face.

She waited until I walked up to the podium and stood behind her before she began to speak. "Thank you for coming to this award ceremony for Detective Alice Liddell. Some of you might be wondering why we would have a ceremony for a routine arrest like the one the detective performed when she brought in the March Hare."

My eyes focused on the back of the room, where multiple cameras filmed the events, and in front of them, reporters waited patiently to ask questions.

"I contend, though, that there was nothing routine about what Detective Liddell did. No, what she did was an act of heroism. So rarely are we allowed a second chance to make amends from our mistakes, and that is exactly what Detective Liddell did by capturing the criminal who got away, and that is worthy of celebration."

She took a deep breath and tugged at the ribbon on the podium in front of her. "In addition, I want the whole of Wonderland to know that I stand behind the NARCOs, and I stand behind Alice Liddell. Everyone should be allowed to make mistakes and should be allowed the ability to atone for them. Detective Liddell might have a lot to atone for still in your eyes, but she has my support and the support of the whole city behind her."

She turned around and pulled a purple ribbon from the podium in front of her. "That is why I present this medal of valor to you, Detective Liddell. We are the many."

"We are the many." The medal was heavy around my head, at least double the size of my badge. It glittered gold, with a flock of small parrots embedded inside of it, the symbol of the Lories. "Thank you."

She waved her hand to the podium. "If you would like to say a few words, the floor is yours."

I wobbled up to the podium. "I…never thought I would do anything worthy of an award." I looked down at Dormouse, who sat in the front row. "I'm not sure I deserve this one, but this has been a hard couple of months, and being embraced by all of you—it means the world to me. I swear I will do better every day of my life to protect this city."

With my statement over, I turned back to Councilwoman Lane. "Oh, that's it? Very well, then how about some questions."

Hands raised all over the room, but then a shriek went out above everyone. "You killed my boy!"

A woman rose from the middle of the crowd and rushed the stage. I recognized her as the young boy's mother, the one I killed, only as she threw a can of red paint on me, splattering all over my black uniform, as I braced forward to protect the councilwoman. I didn't understand that she was after me until it was all over.

A half dozen officers swarmed her before she hit the ground. They may hate me, but an attack on one of us is an attack on us all. We believed that above all else, even our duty to protect those we serve.

I looked down at my body, covered in red, and all I could think of was the poor woman's son, covered in blood, as he cried out in pain, dying in that alley. I shook as the tears fell from my eyes, and I fell to the ground, hyperventilating, gasping for air.

# CHAPTER SEVENTEEN

Councilwoman Lane scooped me off the floor and brought me through a pair of doors hidden inside the wood panels while the police officers carted that poor woman off to a holding cell in the City Hall basement. I couldn't fully comprehend what point she was trying to make, but if her goal was to break me down and have a panic attack, then she accomplished her aims with flying colors.

"In here," Councilwoman Lane said as we entered a large office on the other side of the long corridor. "I use that door sometimes to steal myself away from the press on particularly awful days."

I had never been inside an office so grand before. The floor was a pristine white, and the emblem of the city had been emblazoned in the center of it. Large windows rose twenty feet into the air, and the light from them fell on a long, thick wooden desk carved with roses along its base. Bookcases lined every wall with leather books filling them to capacity.

"Thank you." The trail of red paint had followed me down the hallway and now stained the councilwoman's pristine floor. "Oh my gods, I'm so sorry."

She held up her hand. "Please, it's okay. I spill on it twice a week. The cleaning staff are well equipped to handle any matter of mess." She pointed to a door on the far side of the room. "There's a private washroom in the back there. You should be able to fix yourself up."

I rushed to the door and pulled off my shirt and pants, leaving myself in nothing but my underwear, and it took me a minute to remember the most powerful woman in the city was on the other side of the door. When I realized it, I was mortified.

"Can I call my sister to bring me some clothes?" I asked from behind the door, trying to hold in my shame.

"Of course," she replied. "Just tell her to bring them to room 137."

I made the call and spent precious minutes convincing my sister I was okay before dispatching her to find a clean change of clothes I kept in the trunk of my car for overnight stakeouts.

"If you look behind you, I have a robe," the councilwoman said from the other side of the door. "It's not much, but you are free to wear it until your clothes arrive. Of course, if you would rather hole yourself up in my bathroom, that would be okay, too."

I turned around to find a blue terry cloth robe emblazoned with the seal of Wonderland hanging next to a small shower covered with a glass door. I pulled the robe off its hanger and opened the door. Before I walked outside, I knelt and pulled the medal off my uniform. I didn't want to chance losing it, even though it was still stained with red paint.

"I think that uniform is ruined," I said.

"If you leave them, I can have my staff fix them right up for you. Unfortunately, it is not the first time they have had to deal with a paint bombing."

"It happened to you?" I asked, wide-eyed.

She nodded. "On the campaign trail a few years ago, and again the year before I was elected. My team did all they could to suppress the story. I think it made page twenty of some papers, and we managed to keep it off all but the local news, which was a feat of sheer genius. Seeing a city council candidate covered in paint is quite the image, and that we were able to convince them not to run with it for a week was when Poppy cemented her use to me."

"I could use some of that PR now," I said. "I'm going to be a laughingstock."

She shook her head. "I don't think you should be too quick to dismiss this kind of publicity. Until this moment, you have been the predator or the vigilante, but now you are a victim. Very few people can sympathize with a woman who kills a child and gets away with it, and while they can cheer for a cop who arrests a criminal, nobody can empathize with that either. But now, as a victim, you have been humanized in a way you never could otherwise. That woman did you a great favor."

I looked down at my paint-stained hands. "It doesn't feel like that."

"No, it won't until you look at it in hindsight. There are plenty of things I thought were career killers that my team spun to my advantage."

"Spin." I looked down at the paint dug into my fingernails, even after trying to scrub them clean. "So, is everything politics to you, then?"

"Is everything policework to you?" She held up her hand to stay my answer. "Don't answer that. I know the answer already. Nobody would work as hard as you did to get back on the force if the work didn't consume them. We are what we do, Miss Liddell, and especially what we do well. That is what I admire about you. What I do well is politics, so yes, it clouds everything I do."

"Then tell me why you chose to honor me today. It sounds like career suicide to me."

"I stuck up with you with the council, but I was outvoted. This was a way to get back at them, maybe." She turned toward her desk and walked to the window. "But also, I know an opportunity when I see one, and you are one of the few people on the force who actually seems to want White Rabbit off the street."

Her words burned the inside of my throat. I assumed she honored me because of the Caterpillar, but it seemed her efforts were nobler than that.

"And that's the only reason. Nobody told you to honor me?"

She chuckled. "Quite the opposite. I have received plenty of letters and calls demanding your head, but I see something in you. Something that dies in most NARCOs I meet."

I stepped toward her. "And what is that?"

She turned to me. "Hope."

Before I could ask a follow-up question, there was a knock on the door, and Poppy shuffled inside, taking no notice of me. "There is a woman outside who claims she has clothing for your guest."

"Thank you, Poppy. Show her in."

"Of course, ma'am." She bowed low, completely deferential in a way she was not to my sister or me. Then, she spun on her heels and rushed outside without shutting the door. A moment later, my sister appeared in the door. "Alice! You're all right!"

She wrapped me in a hug as my breathing became labored once again. "I wouldn't go that far, but I'm alive and with no bruises or anything. What happened to that boy's mother?"

Dinah handed me a bag filled with wrinkled clothing. "She was arrested, of course."

"They have her confined in the jail downstairs, no doubt, for questioning. We need to figure out how she was able to sneak a paint bucket into the room without us noticing."

I walked back to the backroom. "I doubt she brought it in. I'll bet it was left there for her."

"That would mean it was an inside job," Councilwoman Lane said. "I hate to think that is the case. I know the ceremony was not looked upon favorably, but that would be outright insubordination."

"My sister is rarely wrong," Dinah said as I passed her.

"I think that poor woman who lost her son would say otherwise," I replied, grabbing the clothes from her.

"That is why I said rarely," she replied softly.

I closed the door to the bathroom and dropped the robe. These weren't my favorite jeans, but they were fine, and I didn't mind getting them dirty. I threw on an old T-shirt, faded with time, that I got at my first concert for Johnny and the Cruisers. I dropped my hair to get the flecks of paint out of it, pulled it back in a ponytail, and grabbed the badge from the uniform, along with my gun. Then, I walked back into the office.

"I want to see her."

"I don't think that's a good idea," Councilwoman Lane said.

Dinah turned to her. "I don't agree with your views on just about anything else, Councilwoman, but I agree with that for sure. You melted into a puddle last time you saw her."

I stepped forward. "She didn't commit any crime unless I press charges, and before I let her get arrested, I need to talk with her." I sighed. "It's something I should have done a long time ago, but I couldn't bring myself to look at her. Now I don't have a choice."

"I still advise against it," Councilwoman Lane said.

I smiled at her. "I appreciate that and everything you've done for me, but this is something I have to do." I clasped the medal closely in my hand. "I hope you know how much your support means to me, though."

"I do," she said. "And you still have it, despite your foolish decision to confront your attacker."

"I ruined her life first."

# CHAPTER EIGHTEEN

The satellite office of the NARCOs was located in the basement of City Hall, close to the records office. They kept a small holding cell for criminals waiting to be brought to jail, and a pair of desks. The room was big enough to make everyone moderately uncomfortable on a good day, but with a dozen officers lining the hallway and crammed inside the room trying to listen to Dormouse's interrogation, it was claustrophobic as all hell.

"How did you get the paint into City Hall?" Dormouse growled from in front of a pair of officers that unintentionally guarded the door with their bodies as they looked in on the proceedings.

"Excuse me." I tapped the bigger of the officers on the shoulder. He turned with scorn, but his face fell when he saw mine, still partially covered with paint. "Can I get inside?"

It wasn't like the uniforms to bend to my requests, and I often had to get Dormouse to mediate between us, but even they must have had some sympathy for a disgraced officer because he tapped his friend, and they both allowed me to enter the small room without a fuss. When I came into view, Dormouse stopped berating the poor woman and turned to me.

"You shouldn't be here," he said, jumping up.

"She attacked me." I turned to her, but her eyes didn't meet mine. "Don't I have the right to speak to my attacker?"

"Of course. I just thought—well, after the incident…"

I held up my hand. "It's okay. I'm okay—no, that's not true, I'm far from okay, but I need to do this."

He nodded and gestured for me to take his seat across from the woman. My hands shook as I turned to her. I had interrogated hundreds of perps over my long career, but I never had the fear that speaking to this woman elicited in me.

Her gaze could not avoid mine when I was across from her, so she had no choice but to meet my eyes then. I had seen the woman before, at my hearings, and on the news. She wore her hatred on every line of her face. The weight of losing her only son weighed on her shoulders and caused her to droop in her seat.

"Do you feel better?" I asked after a long silence. Every eye bore into me, waiting for me to make a hard move, but I was all out of them. I had nothing but sympathy for the woman.

"I'm not ever gonna feel better until you're dead, or I am."

"Your name is Grace, right?" I never said the name out loud or acknowledged it before, even though I read it in police reports, and she spoke against me at my trial.

"You know it is, just like you know my son's name is"—she bit her lip to stop the tears filling her eyes from falling—"was Vincent."

"Of course." I nodded slowly. "I get it, you know. You expected some sort of justice for your boy, and instead, not only did I get off from any punishment, but I got an award. I'll be honest; I don't think that would have ever happened if I hadn't killed your son."

She sneered. "You should rot in hell."

"I agree." I took a long breath. "But before then, I have a lot to do to make amends for what I did to your son. I know you don't believe me, and that's your right. Some people, well, there's nothing you can do to make up for the wrong you did to them. I don't expect forgiveness, but I do forgive you. I'm going to make sure this whole thing goes away."

"I don't care what you do. Send me to jail for the rest of my life for all I care. It's not like I have a whole lot left to live for."

I shook my head. "Your boy, Vincent, wouldn't want you to think like that. There's nothing I can say to get you over that pain, but only you can channel it into something productive. I think Vincent would like that."

Grace swirled the words in her mouth before spitting on me. "Don't you ever use his name. You have no idea what he wanted. You don't get to tell me what to do."

I let the long loogie drip down my face for a moment before wiping it off with the bottom of my shirt. "You're right. I have no right, but I have the right to live and try to make amends, just like you have the right to live. I will never forget what I did to Vin—to your boy. It will haunt me every day of my life. I have no doubt there are plenty of people in Wonderland who want me gone, too. Who knows? Maybe someday you will all have your way, and I'll be run out of town or worse, but until then, I have work to do, and I can't have you mucking that up. Are we going to have a problem?"

"We already have plenty of problems," the woman said. "But I said my piece. You don't gotta worry about me anymore."

"I will worry about you, Grace. If I were a praying woman, you would be in my prayers, but you'll be in my thoughts." I turned to Dormouse. "Let her go. I'm not pressing charges."

"Are you crazy?" Dormouse said. "She assaulted an officer. I can't—"

"Of course, I'm crazy!" I shouted, rising from my chair. "Have you not been paying attention?"

"That's not—"

"I don't care what you meant. Assault isn't a felony, which means it's still my choice if I press charges, and I'm telling you to let her go."

Dormouse stepped forward. "I can classify this as a felony against the state, and then it's not on you."

I hadn't thought of that. "We—I caused this woman enough grief. If you press charges, it will bring more tragedy on this family."

"And what if she comes after you again? What if she interferes with an investigation? What if she hurts somebody else?"

"Then that will be on my head, too. Please don't take that choice away from me."

Dormouse clenched his teeth together. "I'll do what I can, but it's up to the captain. If I let her go and this creates a streak of vigilantism, then it's on your head, and you'll make a lot of enemies if that's the case."

I shrugged. "I already have a lot of enemies. What's a few more?"

# CHAPTER NINETEEN

Dinah met me at the bottom of the stairs. The basement was crowded and not welcoming, so she decided to wait somewhere that she could be helpful without being a nuisance. She brought me home and helped clean the paint out of my hair.

"Maybe you should cut it off."

My eyes lit up, and a thrill of exuberance filled my body at the thought of it. "Yes, that's exactly what I need."

"I was just kidding," she said.

"I know, but I'm not," I replied. "I have a pair of scissors next to the stove and then use an electric razor to get it the rest of the way."

I hated my hair. I hated everything about myself, but every time my hair brushed my neck, I was taken back to the moment I pulled that trigger, and it caused me to lock up and my chest to collapse in on itself.

"This is crazy," Dinah said. "I'm not a barber. There are other people—"

I stood from the bathtub and walked over to the stove. I pulled open my junk drawer and grabbed a pair of scissors before scampering back to her. "I am so serious right now. I need to get this hair off me. Please."

Dinah sighed. She had been my sister my whole life, so she knew it was best to placate me when I got a wild hair up my ass, even if I regretted it later. "You're going to regret this later."

"Maybe."

She didn't make any other objections. She simply grabbed the biggest wads of hair and cut them down as far as she could, but I could see how much it pained her. Dinah cared so deeply about her appearance, waking up hours before her kids to get ready for the day—gods forbid anybody saw her at anything less than her best.

I wasn't like that, though. My appearance didn't matter to me. Any last shred of vanity I had was stripped away by the endless parade of articles with my face on them, each looking more haggard and worn down than the last…and I had another one coming tomorrow, which would wear me down even further. No matter what the councilwoman said, having a public breakdown wouldn't make me look good or restore anybody's faith that I should be entrusted to protect the city. I had to claw and scrape for every inch I ever got, and now it felt like sliding back to the bottom again.

"There," she said after finishing with the scissors. "Now, I have to buzz you because this looks worse than anything I've ever seen."

This wasn't my first time with short hair. I went through a punk phase in college and kept it short through university until I made it through the police exam. Dinah flinched when the buzzer started and held a pained look on her face as she moved the buzzers over my head.

With every single stroke of the buzzer through my hair, I felt my confidence bloom again. Whoever that woman was who followed me around the last few months, she was dead now, and a new, stronger, more powerful Alice emerged from her ashes. I smiled when she was done, and I watched the hair circle the drain with the red paint. It was as if I killed that poor woman who had dealt with so much tragedy, and she bled out at my feet.

"I hope you enjoyed that," Dinah said, looking at her watch. "Because now I'm going to be late picking up James."

I rubbed my head in the mirror as the rest of the bleeding water dripped from my naked body. I hadn't seen a genuine smile on my face in a long while, and seeing it was as jarring as it was freeing. "It's perfect."

"You're a freak," Dinah replied, walking toward the door. "Get therapy. Also, I love you."

"I love you, too. And I think I have therapy tomorrow, actually."

"Then you are smart to preemptively listen to your sister."

# CHAPTER TWENTY

"I see that you found a way around my recommendation to get back out into the field." The headshrinker tapped his fountain pen against a yellow legal pad. "I can't say I'm surprised. You seem like the type. I'm just disappointed."

"I can live with disappointment, Doc," I replied. "As long as I get to be out there. Disappointment is kind of my baseline these days."

"And tell me…" He drew out a long silence. "How does it feel to be back in the field?"

"It feels great."

The therapist pursed his lips and pulled a newspaper from beside his chair. He threw it on the coffee table between us, and it folded open to reveal a picture of me on the front page, in glorious color, showing me lying on the ground covered in red paint. The headline read: *Embattled Officer Doused with Paint at Award Ceremony.*

"This doesn't look great to me. It says in the first paragraph that you had a panic attack. Have you been having them often?"

I looked down at my shaking hands. This morning I woke up feeling like my head would float off into space if I didn't lasso it to my body. "Only when somebody throws paint on me."

His eyes narrowed. "Is this the first time you have been in a confrontation since the incident?"

I shook my head. "No, I had to talk to a perp's mother the other day, too. It wasn't pleasant, but I got through it."

"Explain to me how you felt during that moment?"

I chuckled, thinking back to the fact I could barely breathe when the woman brought up my past. "No offense, Doctor, but anything I say can be used against me, and I already got everything I want, so what's the point of even being here?"

He closed his hands over the top of his paper. "Despite your ability to circumvent my recommendations, the department still puts a lot of faith into my work and whether I think you are mentally fit for active duty." He pointed to the gun on my hip. "Or whether I think you should be carrying that sidearm."

I placed my hand on it. "You can pry it from my cold, dead hands."

"I'm not the enemy here. I'm trying to get down to the root cause of your struggles and allow you to work out your issues in a safe place."

"Safe place? How can anywhere be safe if you can tell my captain to put me back on desk duty? No, Doctor. This isn't safe for me, and frankly, I don't think you want it to be. You need it to be a safe place for your boss and your boss's boss, so when somebody like me does their job, and something bad happens, you can say you did something and clear your conscience."

He furrowed his brow and looked back at his notes before speaking calmly. "You were not supposed to chase that criminal through the alley, were you? You were covering for your partner. Isn't that right?"

I felt my head start to buzz. "Watch yourself."

"I'm sorry for stating the facts, but it seems like you weren't doing your job very well even if you hadn't shot that poor child."

I bit my lip. "You're about one second away from me beating you into a pulp."

"Look at yourself, shaking like a leaf." He held up his hand defensively. "Now, do you really think you are in a good enough place to hold that weapon?"

I looked down to see my hand on the handle of my gun, my index finger wrapped around the hilt. I pulled my hand away and nearly leaped out of my skin. "Oh my god."

"It only takes a fraction of a second to make a terrible mistake," the doctor said. "And you are playing with fire. I would recommend desk duty to you again if I thought it would mean anything. However, I'm quite sure it wouldn't. You have friends in high places, after all."

His tone shifted in his last sentence from comforting to accusatory. Now, it was my turn to narrow my eyes. "And what is that supposed to mean?"

He connected with my eyes. His were soft and kind. "It means, watch yourself, Detective Liddell. Not everyone who gives you what you want has your best interests at heart."

I stood. "I think I know my body better than you, Doctor."

He looked at the holster of my gun, then back up to me. "I hope so."

He didn't mention the fact that I nearly shot him a minute ago. From his expression, it hadn't been the first time, and I certainly wouldn't blame anyone for shooting the smirk off his dumb face.

"I am trying to get better," I said to him after a long silence.

"And yet you stood up"—he looked over to the clock on the wall—"when we have nearly half an hour left. Words are simply that until they are put into action."

"You're right." I took a deep breath. "Do you want to know something crazy?"

He picked up his pen. "It is my job."

"I don't think I could even fire this stupid thing if I wanted to." I patted the gun at my hip. "It's the thing I worry about most."

"Yes." He flipped through his notepad. "I remember seeing you haven't passed your gun test, even though you have been reinstated. That's about the oddest thing I have ever seen."

"Like you said, Doc, I have friends in high places."

"Have you talked to your partner about this? After all, it's his life in danger should you falter when you need to."

"Most narcs never discharge their guns on duty, and those that do almost never do it a second time."

"True, but I think you should go to the range and practice anyway. You want it to be a reflex in case you need it, though I hope you never do."

"If I go to the range, will you stop looking at me so judgmentally?"

"I am looking at you the same way I always do. If you feel it is judgmental, then perhaps it's a sign you are doing something worthy of being judged."

I sneered at him. "Or maybe it's because you're judging me."

He shrugged. "That could be it, too."

# CHAPTER TWENTY-ONE

The firing range had always been a comfort to me, even in the darkest times. I started coming when I was a teenager before I could even hold more than a peashooter without dropping it. I helped sweep away the empty cartridges after closing for recycling and ran the register after school. In return, I got to fire rounds way before I was legally allowed to by the laws of Wonderland.

I never jumped at the explosions of gunfire, and things like fireworks never phased me. However, on that first day stepping back into the range, everything made me skitter and hop. The sounds which used to soothe me now caused me to flinch.

"Haven't seen you in for a while, Allie." An old man, missing half his teeth, smiled at me from behind the desk.

"Yeah, Tommy," I replied. "I guess you heard."

He nodded. "Heard, read, and saw. This whole thing—it makes my heart ache for you, kiddo. You were always one of the good ones. The things they are saying about you…well, I am glad you came back to your roots."

Even after becoming a detective, I still came back to Tommy's range at least once a week. It was a constant in my life the way few other things were. It was there through college, and my exams, in a way my parents, or even Dinah, weren't. Tommy was there to listen to everything, and he never judged.

I had avoided coming back since the incident because I couldn't deal with his judgmental eyes. I could handle anyone else being disappointed with me, but not him.

I pulled out my wallet. "Can I buy two cases of rounds?"

"Your money's no good here, kiddo," he said, pulling three cases of shells from under his desk. The NARCOs preferred assigning .22 caliber to recruits, but I insisted on using my own .45, the same one I grew up shooting. They gave a bit of a fuss, but when I aced my shooting exam, they shut up about it.

"I want this place to stay around, Tommy," I replied, putting a fifty on the table. "I don't know what would happen if it went away, so let me help, okay?"

Tommy picked up the cash. "I'm using this to take you out to dinner, kiddo, so I'll accept it. Chinese, okay?"

"That's an acceptable compromise, I guess." I picked up the boxes of shells. "Thanks for always being there for me."

"As long as you keep coming back, I'll be there." He picked up a phone next to him. "Still like orange chicken?"

I nodded. "It's my favorite."

"Go shooting, and I'll have it ready by the time you get back."

I put on a pair of orange headphones and headed into the range. Two other shooters stood at the edge of the range, and every pop of their clips sent a shiver down my spine. I barely made it to my booth without dropping my bullets from all the shaking.

I took the gun out of my holster and removed the clip. I opened the top case and loaded bullets into it. A standard .45 only holds seven bullets and one in the chamber, but I bought the longer mag that fits fifteen, pulling it ahead of the .22 most other officers carried. I had three additional clips on my belt but never needed them.

The act of loading a pistol used to be cathartic for me, but the shaking of my hands made it a futile pursuit. You needed steady hands to press through the recoil of the clip and force it down enough to push a bullet into it. It took me thirty minutes to load three bullets, and only after slicing through my finger twice. I had been relegated to the floor as I wrapped myself from the cut.

"Do you need some help?"

I looked up to see Dormouse. He smiled at me, but I wasn't about to smile back at him. "Here to rescue me again?"

He knelt to my level. "No, you didn't come back after your therapy session, and I know you like coming here."

"You're quite a detective," I said with a vicious bite on the end of it.

He held up his hands. "Why are you so pissed at me? I'm trying to help."

"You're always trying to help, but you can't help this time. There's nothing you can do. I'm broken, and you should find yourself a new partner." Tears welled in my eyes as I looked around to see both of the other men had left already. Somehow, their bullets still rang through my ears, even as a memory. "I'm no good to anyone."

He pulled one of my spare clips and started loading it. His hands were as sturdy as ever. "Is that why you were hiding this from me? Because you thought I would discard you like some sort of moldy bread?"

"No, I kept it from you because I didn't want you looking at me like I was less than." I pointed to his face and the poor, wounded eyes that stared back at me. "Yup, just like that."

He broke off his gaze. "I'm sorry you think I'm such a monster, but I'm trying to help." He handed me the clip. "There you go. And just so you know, I'm not going to leave you. We're partners, for better or worse."

I wanted to say something, but my phone buzzed, ruining my concentration. I looked down to see a message from the Caterpillar. *Need to see you. Now.*

This was my life now, to come running when a drug dealer called my name. I had given up everything I believed in to get back onto active duty, and I wasn't good for anyone, especially not my doting partner.

I grabbed the clip out of his hands and stood. "I have to go."

"What about Chinese? Tommy said he ordered your favorite."

"I—" I didn't wait to finish before I ran off, leaving my boxes of bullets and a stunned Dormouse as I rushed past him and out the front door without saying goodbye to Tommy. I hoped he enjoyed his dinner because I couldn't eat it. I was sick to my stomach about what I had become.

# CHAPTER TWENTY-TWO

My anxiety rose higher and higher the closer I got to the Looking Glass Lounge. When I was out there among the people, investigating cases, even getting awarded for the work I did, it was easy to lose the fact that I was bought and paid for by the Caterpillar, and he could pull the rug out from under me for any reason.

I already knew Aman was on the take, and he could bust me down to uniform at a moment's notice, or worse, put me on a dangerous beat that was sure to get me killed, especially by partnering me with one of the many officers who despised me, which was just about the whole division.

I parked across the street and took several deep breaths to steel my nerves. I watched the traffic ebb and flow like a wave over the course of two hours. I recognized enough of the people walking in and out, athletes, politicians, and police officers both in my division and otherwise, to understand how deep Caterpillar had his tendrils in Wonderland. It was stupid to assume I could fight against it, one little girl against a force of nature.

As I watched the entrance, my phone buzzed. It was another message from the Caterpillar. *Coming, or will you simply watch all day?*

I pushed myself out of the car and dragged my feet into the club. Even in the middle of the afternoon, girls danced on tables, and the powerful of Wonderland filled the chairs speckling the club. Caterpillar was the Red Queen's anointed, and he had taken the mantle with pride.

It didn't take long to find the Caterpillar's hand waving at me from the back of the club. His checkered neon green suit stood out against the dim lighting. I snaked my way through the club, trying to avoid the musk of sweat that seeped off the stage.

"I thought yhou whould never show, my dear," the Caterpillar whispered as I sat across from him. His teeth lit up blue in the ultraviolet light that seemed only to surround his table. He brought a hookah pipe to his mouth and took a large drag before blowing it out into concentric rings, unconcerned I was waiting for him. "Did yhou get a nice vhiew?"

"I'm sorry for keeping you waiting. Surveillance soothes me."

He smirked. "Yhou must know yhour fhriends as whell as yhou know your enemies, I alwhays say. It's only fhair that yhou know me as whell as I know yhou."

"I don't think that's possible," I replied. "You have half of this city on your payroll, and I doubt they would be very forthcoming with information on you if I asked."

"I should hope not, fhor their sake. It whould be a bad invhestment if they gave me up whilly-nilly."

My eyes narrowed. "And you do not seem like the type to make bad investments."

"Does that make yhou happy? That I chooose yhou to make an invhestment in since I am so good at it?"

I shrugged. "I know what I'm worth."

"A pittance, it whould seem." He stopped for a minute to let his words soak in, but I knew what he meant immediately. Compared to other officers, he bought me for next to nothing, and he was all too happy to gloat about it. "Now, dowhn to business. I hear yhou are lhooking fhor yhoung Yin, a whard of mine."

"One of your dealers, you mean."

"Whatever yhou whant to call it, he is ooone of mine, and thus I have a vhested interested in fiiinding him."

"So what, you want me to botch the investigation?"

He shook his head. "Fhaaaar fhrom it. I am interested in fhinding the boy as much as yhou. He is vhery vhaluable to me, with a bright fhuture. If he whent rogue, I whant to know why."

"He's never caused any trouble for you before, has he?"

"Noooo." Caterpillar picked at the table in front of him as he took another toke of his hookah. "He's alwhays been a model emphloyee. I believe somebody is trying to bring undue attention to me."

"That would be stupid, though, wouldn't it, since you own half the city?"

"And the other half whould love to do me in. They hate what I represent."

"And what is that?"

He smirked as he blew a large ring of smoke from his hookah. "Fhreedom fhrom their problems, and a whorld full of whimsy and whonder."

My eyes narrowed. "You really believe that, don't you?"

He rolled the idea around on his tongue for a moment. "That is not yhour concern. Yhou should only concern yhourself with fhinding Yin and bringing him to the shafhety of my whelcoming bosom."

"I'm already looking for him, so unless you have better information for me, I don't need motivation to do my job." I stood. "Remember this for the future. I don't need to be babied."

Caterpillar reached next to him and pulled a manila folder from the seat. He slid it over to me. "I whouldn't have chosen yhou if yhou wheren't the best. I happen to knoooow the crew he ran whith, as one of my woooomen put it together."

I opened the folder and found printouts of three young men, including Yin, and an older woman, modified to look like a parrot, at least in the feathers around her face, if not in the eyes or mouth…yet.

"Her name is Doreen, bhut I prefer to call her Phigeon. She hates it, which only makes me want to do it moooore."

"I'll go talk to her."

"See that yhou doooo," the Caterpillar said. "Bring my precious ducky home, and yhou whill be rewharded handsomely. If not…whell, I don't need to threaten yhou. Yhou already know what is at stake."

"I don't take kindly to threats anyway. You'll learn that about me soon enough."

"Yhou dooooo have a fire." He closed his mouth in a sullen frown. "Ohne more thing. Keep yhour phartner out of this. He's a dooooo-gooder, and they tend to frowhn on my help."

"He's going to ask questions," I said, matching his scowl.

"Then send him in another direction, my dhear. Use your whomanly whiles on him. Do whatever yhou nheed to, but if he comes into the mix, whell, it whould be quite unpleasant for all of us, but especially him."

# CHAPTER TWENTY-THREE

*Talk to Pigeon, and don't involve Dormouse.* That was going to be hard since he was on my ass even when I wasn't trying to avoid him, and when I was trying to avoid him, somehow, he was even closer to me than that.

The worst part about Dormouse, by far, was that he was a great detective. His brain tied together inconsistencies seamlessly, and it was nearly impossible to get one over on him, and the harder you tried, the more he fought it. Still, if it meant keeping him safe, I had no choice but to do my best, even if it would be a futile effort.

Doreen lived in a nice building in the Antieque district, close enough to her dealers to keep an eye on them but not be seen slumming with them. It could have easily been condemned in another life, like many in Crash Town, except for the care taken in its restoration. The bricks were smooth and glistened in the sun, unlike the cracked and broken ones in the neighborhood I grew up in, and all the windows were pristine and intact, as was the blue awning in front of it where a doorman stood on top of a forest green carpet. Two blocks away this kind of place went for peanuts, but I would bet this was one of the more expensive buildings in Wonderland, even though you could spit on skid row from the penthouse, and I bet they did on occasion.

I walked up to the doorman, who scowled as I approached. I wasn't dressed like one of his customers. Though I wasn't slathered in paint, I was in ripped jeans that weren't intentional, and a duster faded with time.

"I'm here to see Pig—Doreen."

"Last name?" he asked.

Caterpillar didn't tell me. I flipped open the manila envelope and found her picture.

"Richards."

"Is she expecting you?" The doorman had a smug smirk with wrinkles that grooved the sides of his mouth as if it was the only expression he had made for the last sixty years.

"I think so." I pulled out my badge, sick of playing games. "But why don't you ask her?"

His expression changed to one of timid intimidation, and he scooted around his desk to pick up the phone. "Right away, ma'am."

The doorman rang up, and after a few moments, I was inside the elevator riding to the seventh floor. It wasn't the top floor but high enough to be respectable. She would have looks for the next week as word got around that the police came to speak with her.

When the doors opened, a woman with feathers and a beak met me. Since her picture, she must have completed most of her facial reconstruction as all but her eyes resembled that of a parrot, including the brilliant red, blue, and green feathers that plumed from her face and slicked into the back of her head.

"Why did you flash your badge?" she sneered at me. "Do you know what that's going to do to my reputation?"

I held up my hands in defense. "I'm sorry, but your doorman was being a dick. Tell him to be nicer, and I'll be sure not to flash it next time."

She spun on her heels and led me down the hallway. "As if there will be a next time."

In Crash Town, the hallways all looked like they leaked battery acid, with large water spots you could poke through with a light touch. This hallway was different, painted peach with expensive watercolors that hung throughout it and bronze sconces that lit the hall in a soft glow. The best you got in Crash Town was the harsh light of a work light when somebody opened a door to air out the asbestos. But in Antieque, you could do a lot better for yourself.

At the end of the hall, Pigeon opened a white door, and we entered a nice apartment. Nothing too fancy, but every piece was picked special to blend together seamlessly, and the kind of arrogant minimalism that only the rich could get away with, those who never had to worry about being hand to mouth. Those who knew how bad it could get tended to horde everything just in case of an emergency.

"Now, which of my duckies are you trying to find?" she asked, sitting down at a chair that couldn't have been comfortable. She held out her hand. "And be quick about it."

I placed the manila folder in her hand. "Yin, I believe, is his name. He vandalized his aunt's shop and—"

"Please," she brushed me away. "There's no way he did something that stupid. He loved that shop. Yin wanted to own that shop one day. That's why he was working for us, so he could buy his aunt out and give her a way to retire."

"That's actually kind of admirable of him."

She scoffed, preening herself. "You police think people are born bad, but most people, at least the ones I hire, have a reason to sell for us. They have dreams and ambitions. Drugs are a means to an end, not an end in itself."

"That's a noble vision and all, but you hurt a lot of people."

She shook her head. "People begging to get hurt, and those who were hurt way before we got a hold of them."

I took a step toward her. "And what about the people who get strung out on Rabbit and can't go back to their lives? What about the ones who lose their grip on reality?"

"Reality wasn't so good to begin with." She looked up at me. "Did killing that kid make the world safer?"

She was trying to rattle me, and it was working, but I couldn't show it no matter what I did. There was no gaining respect back with somebody like Doreen. If I lost it, then it was gone forever.

"I was trying to do the right thing," I bellowed. "Keeping this junk off the street so nobody can…" She waved me away again. "If you flap your hand at me again, I will break it off and slap you with it."

This caused her to chuckle. "You're funny. Did you know you are funny?"

"Just tell me what you know about Yin and his crew."

She pursed her lips. "He hasn't checked in for a couple of days, and I haven't heard from Chu or Xhang, either. It's not abnormal for a crew to go off the grid for a while after unloading a score and getting paid, so I didn't think anything of it."

"So, they just finished dealing a load for you?"

She nodded. "That's right."

"And how does that work?"

"Really, Detective? Are you that naïve? I thought you were a NARCO." She saw I wasn't going to answer and picked at the feathers on her arm. "Fine, we will go through the motions. They come, I give them a gross of product, and they come back when they're done with the dough, and I give them a cut. Usually, people are pretty wild when they get paid, but Yin was never like that. He was a good kid."

"Except he was a drug dealer."

"Those two things are not mutually exclusive."

"That's true, but it doesn't make them good, either."

"So short-sighted. Were you born that way, or did the academy bang all the nuance out of your skull?"

"Both." I shook my head. "Just tell me where they hung out and what they liked to do, and I will track them down."

"We didn't have sleepovers, Detective." She thought for a moment. "But they did gab a lot while they were here about an arcade on the water they liked to deal at after school. That's the best I have for you, but I will give you a word of advice."

"Goodie, just what I need. Life advice from a criminal."

"I quite agree, Detective," she said, ignoring the layers of sarcasm I slathered on thick. "Handle this quickly. If word gets around that we can't take care of our people, it will be bad for business."

# CHAPTER TWENTY-FOUR

Pier 57 was a popular arcade back when I was growing up, which meant that by now, it was ancient by teenager standards. It had been built on one of the biggest piers on the harbor to look like an old boat. Every room inside the old barge was filled with different arcade games, and even more were housed in the "boathouse" on the dock. Kids had been using it to deal drugs, get high, and skip school for as long as I remembered. It was the perfect place to hide out because there were plenty of tiny nooks to steal yourself away, and the attendants didn't care what you did as long as you came back to the boathouse every couple of hours and bought more quarters.

The dock smelled like dead mackerel and raw sewage, a potent combination that grew worse over the years. The plant that supplied power to half the city dumped toxic sludge into the water, and every election cycle, some politician promised to fix it, but they were empty promises.

I had my own dalliances with the boat when I was younger, but my eyes were always on the future, which meant I never partook of the myriad illegal activities a youngster could get into if they weren't so dutiful as I was in those days.

The name on the badge might have changed, but the same pimply-faced kids manned the register in the boat house as they did when I was young. Their names were Heather and Jack now, instead of Charles and Ynez when I was a kid, but they could have been the perkier ghosts of their former incarnations.

"Good afternoon," Heather said with a lisp from her braces. "Welcome to Pier 57. Ready to set off to adventure?"

"You have way too much energy, Heather," I growled. A quick nod from Jack told me he agreed that she was a bit too much. "I'm looking for somebody."

"We can't give out any information on guests," Jack said. "It's against the rules."

I pulled out the manila folder and placed my badge on top of it. "I think we're beyond that, Jack. Now—" I opened the folder. "Have you seen any of these boys around recently?"

Fear filled their faces as they looked down at the three boys' pictures in the file.

"Are—are they in trouble?" Heather asked.

"Does dealing drugs count as trouble?"

They both gasped. Jack narrowed his eyes. "I told you that you shouldn't have hooked up with them!"

"I only hooked up with one of them!" Heather shouted back. "You make me sound like a whore!"

"Calm down." I waited until it was quiet, even if the nervous tension was palpable. "Now, which one did you hook up with?" I pointed to Yin. "Was it this boy?"

She shook her head. "No, it was Chu. He's the cute one."

"Point him out," I said, sliding the folder toward her. "The cute one doesn't help me at all."

She pointed to the boy in the center. He was the only one smiling in his picture. The others looked like mug shots, and likely they would be in jail before long if they weren't careful and if they weren't already dead.

"Was it worth it?" Jack acted disgusted.

Heather looked back at him. "Please, like you didn't let Yin fondle your junk last year."

"Yeah, that was before he started dealing!" Jack shouted.

"Okay, good!" I shouted. "You both knew he was a drug dealer. Then you can both help me."

"Oh my god," Heather said. "You're not going to arrest me, are you? I didn't know that was illegal."

"Relax. I just need some information. Now, where exactly did they hook up with you? At their house, at yours?"

"Neither." Jack sighed. "There's a room in the boat that we—that we use whenever we…you know. It has a mattress and everything."

"And is anyone using that room right now?" I asked, hand moving to the gun on my hip.

Jack and Heather's eyes darted at each other, then forward, and then toward the ship before they each took a long, deep breath.

"It's not our fault," Heather said. "We're not, like, harboring a fugitive or whatever, are we? He just needed a place to stay, and he paid us, so…"

Something slammed on the dock and caused the boathouse to shake. I rushed out, holding my pistol in my hand as I watched a black-haired boy rush off toward the end of the dock. "Freeze!"

I raised the gun, and it shook in my hand. I couldn't get off a good shot if I tried, and as my finger rose from the trigger, I knew that I couldn't try even if I wanted to. I holstered the gun and rushed forward.

The boy leaped down from the dock onto the sand and rolled into a sprint. I wasn't so graceful with my jump, and I landed with a thud. I rushed to my feet, my butt and knees sore, and followed the kid along the beach. He was smaller than me but quicker. Every step I took, he took three, and was pulling away from me.

"Stop!" I screamed as we raced up the stairs to the street. As we climbed them, he tripped and twisted his ankle. He rose with a hobble, and for the first time, I had the upper hand.

By the time we reached the top of the stairs, we were neck and neck with each other, and I took a running leap, lunging forward and grabbing the boy's legs. He tripped and slammed into the ground with a thud.

"Don't resist!" I spun him over, expecting Yin or Chu, but found neither of them. He was just some scared boy.

"Don't kill me," he said, flinching his arms to his face. "I didn't take it, I swear."

"What are you talking about?"

"The Rabbit." Tears streamed down his face as he babbled through his cries. "I swear it wasn't me."

"My gods, this is pathetic." I pulled the boy to his feet. Now I recognized him as the third in the group of dealers I was tracking down. "What are you, thirteen?"

"Fourteen."

He was already broken. Yelling at him wouldn't do a thing, and playing the tough guy would make him curl up more and might even cause him to shut down completely.

"You look terrible," I said, brushing him off. "When was the last time you ate?"

He looked at me, confused. "I—I don't know. I had a candy bar this morning."

"I mean really eat—you know what, come on. I'll get you a burger, and you can tell me everything."

# CHAPTER TWENTY-FIVE

The boy ate like he hadn't touched food in a month. I did get that his name was Xhang, and he was the newest member of the triad that made up their squad. Of course, those things I already knew from the dossier, but I still acted like it was new information. The more information you teased out of a suspect, the easier it was to get more and more, like drilling a small hole in a dam and watching it crack further and further until the whole thing collapsed.

"Are you satisfied now?" I asked Xhang as he swallowed his third burger nearly whole.

"Can I—get a milkshake?"

"Fine." I waved over the waitress and put in the order before turning back to him. "Now, you need to tell me what happened."

He sighed. "I don't want to get anyone in trouble."

"Kid, all of you are in so much trouble right now it's hard to imagine how you could get into more if you tried. I'm trying to help you, but if you can't help me, I'll just take you back to Caterpillar and let him have at you."

His eyes went wide. "You know Caterpillar."

"He's the one who sent me on this goose chase for you in the first place. And trust me, that is not the type of man you want knowing your name."

"Shit, shit, shit, shit, shit. We are so fucked."

I slammed my hand on the table. "Why don't we start with you? If we can get you unfucked, then maybe we can worry about the others."

He held up his hands. "Okay, okay. It wasn't my idea, okay? It was all Yin and Chu. I swear my life went downhill the minute I met those two."

"I think your life went downhill the minute you became a drug dealer, but—"

"No, that's where you're wrong." He shook his head as he stuffed a fistful of fries into his mouth. "Doreen saved me, man. She gave me a chance to get out of my shitty house and live on my own."

I raised an eyebrow. "When I found you, you were living in an arcade."

"I know, cool, right?" His smile was beaming. "That's the dream, man."

He really was just a little kid. "Let's get back on task here."

"Right, right. So, you know we work for Caterpillar, right?"

"I would assume that's why he sent me after you."

"But he's not the only game in town. Yin thought it was a good idea to double up and start working for another dealer. Said they paid better."

I narrowed my gaze. "Was it a fuzzy bunny?"

He pointed at me with a fry dipped in ketchup. "No, I heard of that guy, though. He sucks. No, this one is called the White Queen."

"Original," I replied. "So, I assume this new queen has the intention of taking over the Rabbit trade in Wonderland then?"

"Don't they all?" He realized the snideness of the remark and bit his tongue. "Sorry, it's just that, yeah, I'm on edge 'cuz of the Caterpillar hiring you to track me down."

"He actually wanted me to find your friend, Yin, and now I think I know why. So, Yin and Chu decided to deal for the White Queen. Then what happened?"

"Everything went to hell, didn't it? Yin met with the White Queen and got a load, but then Chu had a change of heart and wanted to tell the Caterpillar what happened. He thought they would take pity on us if we were honest, but Yin thought he would kill us if he found out. They got into a fight, and Chu ended up dead, man. Yin freaked out and wanted to leave town, but he knew people would be after him, so he trashed his aunt's store. He took the Rabbit and booked it, man. The White Queen did not like that, and she's been after me." The anxiety rose in his words as he kept going, and by the end, he had grabbed at his hair and was pulling on it. "And now the Caterpillar's after me, too. Fuck man! Fuck me!"

"Shh," I said, trying to calm the poor boy down. "You've made some shit for yourself, but I'm going to make it right if I can. Come with me, and we'll go talk to the Caterpillar together."

He slammed his hands on the table. "Fuck no, man. I'm not going there."

I gritted my teeth. "That wasn't a question. You can either come talk to the Caterpillar, or you can go to jail, and I promise you he'll find you in jail, and it won't be pleasant. If you come with me, at least you might live through the night."

"I—I don't like the way you said might."

"I don't either, but I don't peddle in false hope." The waitress brought the milkshake to the table. "Now, drink your shake, and then we'll go."

He drank the shake as slowly as humanly possible. For a person who wolfed down three cheeseburgers in less than ten minutes, spending an hour nursing a shake was excessive. Eventually, I forced him to get a to-go cup and stuffed him in my car.

"If you spill that on the seat, I'll kill you myself."

The tension in my gut didn't subside when I reached the Looking Glass Lounge, but now I had a purpose, which trumped my anxiety. I pulled Xhang from the car and into the lounge. He was a child, and when he saw the dancing women, his eyes went wide.

"Come on," I growled, pulling him forward with what remained of his milkshake.

I dragged him through the floor to the back, where the Caterpillar still sat, and threw him down on the booth next to him.

"And whooooo is this?"

"Xhang is what he told me. He's one of Yin's people."

"Funny, I dooon't recognize him. Must have that kind of fhace."

I shrugged. "You'll have to trust me since I lost the file you gave me at the pier."

The Caterpillar turned his glassy eyes to the boy. "And yhou whorked with my little Yin, is that right?"

Xhang gulped. "I—I did, but I didn't do anything, honest."

"Does that mean yhou don't know where my whaywhard duckies are, Xhang?" He spoke slowly, enunciating every syllable. "Because if yhou do, aaand you didn't tell me, I whill take that as a major slight against me.

Of cooourse, if hyou dhon't, then it won't go much better for yhou."

"Go easy on the kid, okay? If he thinks he's doomed, either way, he's not going to say anything."

The Caterpillar snapped his neck to me. "And who are yhou to tell me how to rhun my business?"

"I'm the dirty cop on your payroll who wants to resolve this without any bloodshed." I remembered Chu was dead. "I'm trying to help you, but I am still a cop first and your errand girl second."

The Caterpillar groaned slightly. "Vhery whell. Then answher me this, Xhang. Where is the White Queen's headquarters?"

"I don't know. I didn't go to the meeting with her. Yin and Chu—that was all them. I didn't want to sell that skunk Rabbit, Mr. Caterpillar. I swear it, and I would've told you sooner, but Chu—and then when he died…I panicked."

"I understand, whelp." He sighed and leaned back in his chair, then motioned for two guards by the door. "Unfhortunately, if that is the case, then yhou have noo use to me."

"Wait," I replied. "What if he can show me where Chu's body is?"

Caterpillar rocked in his chair, holding up his arm to stay the guards from moving closer.

"That whould be something, but yhou whouldn't be trying to stall me, whould yhou?"

"Of course, I am. You're about to kill a kid, and I don't need that on my conscience. If you wanted somebody on your payroll who would be okay with that kind of thing, you should have recruited a different cop because that's not me."

"Ooooh, I know that all too whell, which is why I whanted yhou in the fhirst place." Caterpillar stroked his chin. "If yhour new fhriend can show me where Chu's body is, then I whill let yhour new fhriend live, but this is nhot ovher. I whant Yin, and I whant the White Queen. Understood?"

I nodded. "You'll have them both, but if you kill Xhang, or Yin, or anybody else, and I find out about it, I'm done, and I'll dedicate the rest of my life to taking you down."

He smiled. "It whill be a short lifhe."

"I have no doubt, so I'll have to work fast." I pulled Xhang from the chair. "Come on. We have things to do."

As we walked off, it was me who Xhang looked at with stars in his eyes, even as the girls danced around him. "Wow, you told off the kingpin. You must have balls of steel."

"I don't have balls, kid. Balls shrivel at the slightest touch. Now, a vagina. That takes a pounding, and yes, mine is made of steel."

"Gross," he said as we passed through the door into the street.

"What? Balls aren't gross, but vaginas are? What humans are you looking at?"

"Enough! This is gross." He threw his hands in the air in such a way that he spilled what remained of his milkshake on his head. "Oh, man."

"That's what you get," I said with a chuckle. "I have a towel in the trunk. Don't get any of that on my seats, or I will quite literally rip your balls off."

# CHAPTER TWENTY-SIX

I followed Xhang's directions to the front of an abandoned warehouse on the outskirts of town. My jurisdiction to investigate was sketchy at best, but I doubted that Caterpillar would accept my hesitance or a technicality. He seemed like the type who wanted results at all costs, and if I didn't deliver, Xhang was as good as dead.

"What is it with kids and abandoned buildings?" I asked when I put the car into park. "They're not as cool as you think they are."

"Yeah, well, I live in a 600-square foot apartment with three brothers, a sister, and my parents. Having some silence and a little breathing room seems pretty cool to me."

"Fair enough."

The smell hit me when I exited the car like a burly man socked me in the gut. Standing out among the other smells around the shithole was something else because there were plenty of dogs and cats that used the area for a personal litter box, not to mention the homeless, several of which I spotted hunkered in other buildings as we neared.

The whole area was once owned by the Red Queen but was sold at foreclosure when she went to prison. It was supposed to be a brand-new development of houses, but when nobody bought, the developers turned it into business warehousing. Nobody wanted to piss off the Red Queen enough to move in once the warehouses were finished, and eventually, the whole lot went fallow, and the developers went bankrupt. We called it the Skid.

"I don't wanna go in there," Xhang said, quivering his lips in a way that made him seem every bit the child he was.

"Tough, you should have thought of that before you started dealing drugs and took up with criminals. Now, show me the body."

I pulled a dirty shirt out of the trunk and used it to cover my nose from the smell. Most NARCOs wanted to work in homicide, but I preferred vice because you rarely had to deal with dead bodies. My stomach had a strong constitution, but the smell was more than I could handle. I was lucky I didn't eat anything at the diner earlier, even more so when Xhang doubled over and vomited halfway through the building.

I held my hand to my mouth and willed myself not to vomit with him, but I couldn't hold it against the kid. It was a nauseating smell, and the sight that accompanied it moments later was even worse.

Chu was a cute kid in life, but in death, his tongue hung out of his mouth, and his eyes, once full of happiness, were clouded and stared off into the distance. I intended to have Xhang explain what happened, but it was clear from the gash on the back of Chu's head and the blood pooled under his body exactly how he died.

I had to call it in, but before I did, I needed to pick the body clean of anything that could be a clue. I reached into my duster, pulled out a pair of gloves, and slid them on.

"Don't move," I said to Xhang as I stepped over an exposed beam toward the body.

I never met Chu, but he didn't deserve to die in a drug deal gone wrong. Nobody did, especially a kid. My mind immediately went back to the March Hare, and the child I killed died in exactly the same kind of situation, except he was truly innocent, and my hand started to shake, and then my back, violently and uncontrollably.

"Are you okay?" Xhang asked, looking over at me.

I was not okay, and I immediately bolted out of the back of the warehouse and started to take shallow breaths, doubling over on myself. I stayed that way for a moment until I felt a small hand on my back. Xhang bent down and handed me a paper bag.

"In and out. Slowly."

I didn't question. I held the bag to my mouth and did what he said, taking deep breaths in and out until I started to calm down.

"Thanks, kid. That was quick thinking."

"My sister has panic attacks and refuses to take medication. So, it happens, not infrequently."

"Where did you find the bag? You bring them with you randomly?"

Xhang shook his head. "I brought my lunch last time. I just left it here after…"

I looked down at the bag. Xhang was written on it with large, loopy cursive. "Your mom packed you a bag lunch to your drug deal?"

"Hey! It's not like she knew where I was going. I was supposed to be in school, and yeah, she still packs my lunch. What of it?"

I pushed myself to stand. "Just not very criminal of you."

"Yeah, well, I don't wanna be a criminal. Just…fate conspired against me."

I stepped toward him. "I get it. I don't approve of it, but I get it."

And I did. I didn't grow up in much better conditions than Xhang, even though it was a generation ago. My mother, sister, and I lived in a studio apartment, sharing a bed after my dad left. It was not pretty.

I followed my steps back into the room, but after looking through the body, I didn't find anything useful. It was time to call Dormouse, and I absolutely hated making that call. Not only was Caterpillar going to disapprove, but I was in for an earful for going out on my own, and I really didn't like being scolded, especially by him. Of course, he was the only one who could get away with it and not leave with a fat lip.

# CHAPTER TWENTY-SEVEN

"Jesus Christ, Liddell," Dormouse said as he stepped out of the abandoned warehouse toward me. "What did you step into?"

I pointed to Xhang. "I tracked down a lead and found one of Yin's friends. He told me about a fight Yin had with the dead kid that led to the mess you saw inside."

Dormouse eyed Chu as he stepped toward me. "And don't you think it's a little bit convenient that he could pin a murder on a kid who was missing?"

*Shit. I hadn't thought of that. I was rusty. Maybe I shouldn't even be on the force.* Still, I wasn't about to give him the satisfaction. "I believe him."

I had to save face and hope Dormouse believed me. After all, we had been partners a long time, and each followed our instincts more times than we could count. I didn't want to reveal how I knew he was telling the truth. If he knew about Caterpillar, or if Caterpillar knew about my loose lips, that could be the end of everything. Still, this was too much to do on my own.

"I'm the same cop as before, Dormouse. If you believed me then, then believe me now. The kid didn't do it, and now we have a missing person who's the lead suspect in a murder."

Dormouse sighed. "I do believe you. I just wish you trusted me to let me in on this."

"It's not about trust." That was true, to an extent. "It's about getting caught up in a case and following my gut before a trail goes cold. Once I knew I had something, the first thing I did was call you."

Dormouse nodded slowly and turned back to the building where the coroner was wheeling out Chu's body. "We need to take the kid downtown for a statement, and hopefully, the medical examiner will give us a clue about where to find Yin when he examines the body because, as far as I can tell, that place has been wiped clean of clues."

My eyebrow raised. "Wiped, or there weren't any to begin with?"

"I don't know." Dormouse thought about it for a second, rubbing his forehead. "They are kids, right? And by your witness's own admission, they spend a lot of time here?"

"That's right on both counts."

"Then where is the dirt, the muck, the comic books, the old food, and the filth? Where are the dirty magazines and the trash? Not to generalize, but kids are disgusting, and boys even more so."

I hadn't thought about that, either. I rifled through my coat and pulled out the paper bag Xhang gave me. "Here, maybe there's something on this."

"Where did you get that?"

I looked over at Xhang. "I was—having a moment, and he said it was how he packed his lunch the day Chu died."

He looked at the bag. "Did you breathe into this?" He must have seen my face because his voice softened. "It's okay if you had a panic attack, but I need to know."

I nodded. "I did."

He growled under his breath. "Then this will be inadmissible as evidence; you know that."

"Maybe, but it could give us something, anything."

There was nothing else to be learned at the scene, at least not until forensics combed through and collected anything they could from it. Maybe Dormouse couldn't find anything, but he didn't have the equipment to do UV scans and whatever other tests they did to pull evidence from a scene. Still, it was troubling if the scene was wiped down. It meant somebody either came back to it or wiped it down before they left and usually people, especially children, didn't think that well after committing a crime. Of course, most children weren't drug dealers, either.

"Come on, Xhang. Let's go."

I walked Xhang to the car and tossed him in the backseat. I told Dormouse I would meet him back at the station with the kid. I needed some time with the kid to try and get our stories straight and keep Caterpillar out of his mouth.

"Am I under arrest?" Xhang asked weakly from the back seat.

"I don't know. Did you do anything wrong?" His eyes darted away from me. "I mean, besides what you've already copped to."

"You mean did I kill Chu? I can't believe you would ask me that."

"Well, you have to excuse me. After all, we've only known each other a couple of hours, and you're a criminal, so that doesn't put you in the best light."

"And you're corrupt." He said it so matter-of-factly that it took me aback. "Surprised I know what that is?"

I shook my head. "No, you're a criminal. I expect you to know that kind of thing. Still, it's hard to hear it. I don't want to be like that, but I had no choice. If I didn't, well, I don't expect you to understand grown-up things."

"You think I want to deal drugs? I want to go to college and become an accountant, so I can live somewhere better than Wonderland, but I had no choice because it's not like my mom can pay for my school, and I'm not smart enough to get a scholarship."

"Don't say that," I replied. "If you apply yourself—"

"What?" His words were biting and grew more so with each word he spoke. "You're wrong. I can't be the model minority you all expect me to be. You people think you know me. Every year there are stories about poor kids who get scholarships and go to college somewhere amazing. You think that means we're all getting ahead, but that's like a hundred kids out of millions. Most of us don't get those scholarships. Most of us can't work three jobs and still get straight As. That shit is hard—just showing up is hard enough, so please, spare me your bullshit."

"I'm sorry," I said. "But you're wrong about me. I grew up not that far from your house."

"Yeah, in Antieque, I'm sure."

I stifled a laugh. "Yeah, right. No, I was down on Fifth and Cross, about ten blocks from you. Whenever I pass my old block, I'm shocked that my old building is still standing. It should have been condemned twenty years ago. I know what it's like to come from the bottom and what it means to make the hard choices."

"And how did you get out of it?" Xhang asked.

"I'm not sure I did. After all, I still work the same beat. And now, I'm a criminal, same as you. My mom would roll over in her grave."

He leaned forward. "So would my mom, but we have to do what we have to do. If I go to jail, it will kill my mom."

"Don't worry. I won't say anything about the drugs, but if you know anything else about where we can find Yin, you need to tell me. I can't protect you if you don't trust me."

"That's not easy since you wear that badge."

"Yeah, I know, but I promise you my partner will find out. He is dogged, and he's not under Caterpillar's thumb. I've seen him catch a scent and run with it for months, unable to sleep until he put the culprit behind bars. He's going to interrogate you when we get to the station, and if you know something, you'll break. So, you might as well tell me now and give me the chance to cover for you."

He dropped his eyes. "I know the name of his dealer, the one he met with on the White Queen's side. I'll tell you who it is, but you have to promise me something."

"What?"

He swallowed loudly. "You didn't hear it from me."

I looked at him through the rearview mirror. "Hear what from who?"

He cracked a smile. "Exactly."

# CHAPTER TWENTY-EIGHT

Before I brought Xhang to the police station, there was the simple matter of Caterpillar to deal with. He told me explicitly not to call Dormouse, and I not only called him but the entire police department. There was no way he didn't hear about it with all of his connections, and I needed to deal with it head-on before he came for me.

I pulled Xhang from the car and brought him into the Looking Glass Lounge. When I entered, Caterpillar was in front of a small stage, watching a pretty, black-haired woman dance for him. When he turned and saw me, the smile on his face dropped.

"I thought I tooold yhou not to invholve your partner. I whas vhery clear, I believe."

I nodded. "You were, but—" I pulled Xhang forward. "I didn't have many options after Xhang brought me to the scene of a murder. I told you already I'm a cop first and your lackey second."

He stood, pressing his fingers into the bridge of his nose. "I doooon't understand. Yhou knew there whas a murder because I knew there whas a murder, because yhou told me there whas a murder, and yhet you still disobeyed me."

I nodded. "I did what was best for the case."

His face went red. "I DON'T GIVE A FUCK ABOUT THE CASE!" He took a deep breath, and a smile twitched on his face. His true colors had been revealed. Under the outlandish voice and overblown personality, he was Wonderland trash, just like the rest of us. "See what yhou have made me doo? I have lost my composure. Vhery inelegant. Fhorgive me."

"At least now I've seen your true form."

He smiled. "Yhou have seen nothing yhet. Deny me again, and yhou whill see how petty and vhindictive I can be."

I furrowed my brows. "So, does that mean we're okay? Dormouse isn't in any danger."

His smile grew. "He is in imminent danger, my dhear. He is yhour partner, but none fhrom me…as of yhet. Bhut make sure yhour dog doesn't hunt, understand?"

I understood. He meant that I needed to make sure Dormouse stayed off Caterpillar's trail, or it would become a problem, and Caterpillar dealt with his problems with extreme prejudice.

"Thank you," I said while pulling Xhang out of the room.

*I was not a criminal.* I had worked my whole life to put scum like Caterpillar in jail, and I was not a criminal. I was criminal-adjacent, maybe, but one day I would make Caterpillar pay and prove I was never under his thumb, no matter what anybody, including him, thought. I would make all of them pay, and when I had enough evidence, I would turn state's evidence and put them all in jail. It didn't matter if my life would be over after that; I would have done my bit of good for the universe.

I had already learned more in my few days working for Caterpillar than I could have in months working the street. And I had the inside track to stopping the White Queen from leaking her poison onto the street. Yes, taking her down would help the Caterpillar cement his hold on the White Rabbit trade, but for now, we had the same goal. He would eventually, surely, force me to do something nefarious, and I would have to make a tough choice at that moment, but until then, I could hide in the fact that I was taking down bad guys, even if it wasn't exactly how I planned when I was growing up. But then, nothing ever is.

"Are you ready?" I asked when I pulled into the parking garage of the police precinct. I turned back to Xhang. "Remember, don't say a word about Caterpillar. Only bring up the White Queen."

"I know how to lie," Xhang said.

"I'm sure you do, but I still feel the need to tell you once again that the Caterpillar has half the police department on his payroll, and if you say his name, bad things will happen that I can't protect you from."

He looked over at the entrance to the precinct. "If bringing me to a police station is your idea of protecting me, then I think maybe I don't need your protection." He collected himself, taking a deep breath in and out. "I won't say anything to your partner about Caterpillar. Still, it does beg the question: if Caterpillar owns half the precinct, how many of your fellow officers does the White Queen have on her payroll?"

I hadn't thought about that. It was becoming a recurring theme of my life in recent days, things I hadn't thought about. I was rusty. It would all come back to me, like riding a bike. This was just those few wobbly pedals before I got my feet under me and took off down the street.

"Worry about Caterpillar. Let me worry about the White Queen."

I pulled Xhang out of the car and dragged him into the precinct. If Caterpillar told his men not to hurt me, it didn't show in the officer's eyes I passed. They all looked at me with malice and hatred as I strode through the basement where the uniforms hung out and took the elevator up to the bullpen where the detectives worked. My reception was no kinder there, except from Dormouse, who smiled as I walked toward his desk.

"I thought maybe you got lost," he said.

I winced. "I kind of did."

It was a lie, but the white kind that didn't hurt anyone. I needed as much time as possible with Xhang to prep him for his interrogation, and that meant circling the block for fifteen minutes while I drilled him on how to avoid Dormouse's probing questions.

"It's okay. You're just getting back to it."

I sat Xhang down across from Dormouse. "Do you need me? Because I have a lead to follow up on."

"I can handle this," he replied. "If you wait, I can go with you."

"Divide and conquer, Dormouse. Just like the old days."

Dormouse didn't look happy at my answer but a far cry happier than my captain, Aman, when he stepped out of his office and barked across the bullpen at me.

"Liddell! Get in here, now!"

Captain Aman always treated me fairly before my incident, but since then, he had been a ball of fury whenever he looked at me. I thought it might help ease the captain's fury now that I was also on Caterpillar's payroll, but his purple face and veins popping out of his forehead told me that wasn't likely.

"Goddamn it, Liddell," he growled. "It's one thing after another with you. I thought when you came back to the force, I could keep you quiet by feeding you petty cases, but now you're involved in a murder investigation. You are causing me to get an ulcer."

"You already had an ulcer, Cap."

"A bigger one!" he shouted. He took a deep breath. "On top of that, you're on the front page of the paper again. Who lets themselves get doused with red paint?"

"I'm sorry, Captain."

"No, but you will be after this."

My eyes narrowed. "After what?"

He shook his head. "The brass doesn't understand that you are terrible in front of a camera. They will, though, because they are asking you to meet with Vincent's mother and bury the hatchet."

"They want her to bury it in my head? Because that's about the only thing you could convince that woman to do. And besides, I've got cases, so I'll have to pass."

"That's not your choice."

"I think it is, because I made it."

"Goddamn it, Liddell." Aman banged his fist on the table. "If you want to keep having cases, I suggest you don't pass on this." He took a deep breath. "As part of her plea deal, the woman has agreed to a photo op with you to assure everyone in the city that she loves the boys and girls in blue."

"Plea deal?" I asked. "I told her I wasn't pressing charges."

"You don't decide that, Liddell! While you're on the clock, you're one of mine, and I can't have little old ladies getting any ideas about what they can do to my officers. If they get bold, we'll have criminals shooting up my office— do you see how these things can escalate?"

I shook my head. "No, but if this is an order, then I have no choice."

"It is a direct order, and unlike my order to stay home and rest, you had better take this one seriously because if you don't, then it's your head on the chopping block. For good."

I stared at him for a long time. *Did he know I was on Caterpillar's payroll?* Was he yelling at me as a meaningless show of force, or was I really in trouble? If I couldn't maintain my job, then what good was I to Caterpillar, and what would he force me to do then? If I got kicked off the force, what good was I to myself?

"When is it?" I asked.

"It's happening in an hour. I was about to call you and break the news. Thanks for saving me the call." He slid a piece of paper across the table. "There is the location. Don't be late."

I grabbed the paper. "And what would they have done if I refused?"

"Fired you, of course, and made sure to repossess that fancy door we had installed on your apartment to boot so that whoever wants to do you harm would have easy access. So, it's a good thing you didn't say no."

# CHAPTER TWENTY-NINE

I didn't have time for a stupid photo op, but I also couldn't lose my job. I had some level of confidence that Caterpillar would step in to prevent that, but I had never seen the captain like that before. He was always a bit ornery, but anyone who saw what he did in his career, from life during the Red Queen's reign to cleaning up the pieces to adjusting to the new normal, would be the same way. Hell, half of Wonderland was barely hanging onto their sanity by a thread, and the other half dove back into the world of White Rabbit with reckless abandon, willing to die for a taste of the sweet life once again. However, he was also quite sweet and accommodating when he needed to be, or at least he was before the incident. I couldn't let him down, which was why, after stopping by my apartment for a quick shower and a change of clothes, I found myself sitting in front of a small malt shop in the Thread, a horizontal ten-block radius of row homes that separated the north side of Wonderland from the south side. I hadn't been back to it since that night when I killed Vincent, and my whole body shook as I tried to calm myself down.

It took all my power to open the door to my apartment and take a step outside, and now I was supposed to walk into the shop, surrounded by reporters, and pretend everything was okay? And worse, Grace was supposed to look me in the eyes and say she didn't hate me?

Before I could get the nerve, I heard a tight rap on my window. I turned to see Poppy standing outside in a pink dress, holding a clipboard. Her face was too orange for a natural tan, and her teeth were too white to be made that way. I hadn't noticed it in the low light of City Hall, but in the light of day, it was all I could focus on.

"Well, howdy," Poppy said as I opened the door. "You must be Detective Alice Liddell. My name is Poppy, and I'm the press secretary for Councilwoman Lane. She set up this whole event, and we are just so happy you could make it."

Of course, this came from the councilwoman's office. I was assaulted on her watch, after all, and perception was everything to her. It also made sense why Aman was so stressed. It wasn't just the police chief breathing down his neck to make it right, but the city council as well.

"Yes, Poppy. We met a couple of days ago."

She cocked her head. She clearly met a lot of people, and they left her head as quickly as they entered. "Oh yes, so we did. Well, come on then."

My hands still shook, but I willed myself out of the car and put one foot in front of the other as I followed her around the building and into a back door in the alley behind it.

"Now, I know I don't have to tell you, but the press doesn't like cursing, and they love conflict. Whatever you do, don't give them either. They are expecting one or both of you to blow up or break down, so if you can avoid doing either, that would be great, but if you can't, then at least try not to blow up, okay?"

"I'll do my best, but I don't think I'm the one you have to worry about."

She held up her hand. "We have already talked to Grace. She'll be fine. It was a moment of impulse in an otherwise calm and sedated life."

I narrowed my eyes. "She brought that paint into City Hall and waited for the right moment to throw it. Have you figured out how she got it into the building anyway?"

Poppy pursed her lips. "I'm sure I don't have to tell you there are many people who don't like you and sympathize with her. Needless to say, we have found the culprit and dealt with them, but we are hoping that after today it won't be an issue because everyone will love you again."

I chuckled. "Nobody loved me before. I would rather they forgot about me."

She smiled. "I think that's probably a fantasy, Miss Liddell."

"It's 'detective'," I growled at her.

"Of course." She peeked out into the restaurant.

"Why is it such a fantasy to be forgotten? You forgot me."

"Well, that's true, but I promise I won't forget about you again. Not after today. After all, I am very good at my job."

I caught a glimpse of Grace, sitting on the edge of the counter wearing a powder blue dress, with lace gloves and a small cap pinned to her hair. She looked every bit her namesake, and I suddenly wished I wore something nicer than jeans, a T-shirt, and a leather coat.

"Great," I said with a sigh. "That's just swell."

Poppy nodded, and somebody at the front of the shop raised the blinds, and the photographers started shooting. The flashes were blinding, so I looked down at Poppy's bright pink shoes that clacked along the ceramic floor as we walked forward.

"Miss Grace, it's so nice to see you again. May I present Miss—my apologies, Detective Liddell."

Grace nodded and walked forward to shake my hand. "We have met. Would you care to join me for a malt?"

I smiled, my back tight as I tried to keep my posture. I tended to slouch, and that would make me look more like the monster on camera than people already thought of me.

"That sounds lovely."

"Well," Poppy clapped her hands. "I'll leave you both to it."

She turned as a man in a paper cap brought two vanilla milkshakes toward us. "If you would prefer chocolate or strawberry, please let me know. They said vanilla was the safest bet."

"I'm sure it's fine," I said with a smile, bringing the glass closer to me. "You have a lovely shop."

"It was Vincent's favorite," Grace said with a smile, but the bile beneath her words was palpable. She looked over at the soda jerk. "Thank you, Walter. This is great."

Walter smiled at Grace and then me, though his eyes directed venom behind his false smile as he walked away.

"I'm so sorry about this," I said as he walked away. "I swear I didn't press charges."

She shrugged. "It's what it is. It was made clear that I don't have the power here, and if I don't play ball, my life will be made a living hell. Of course, it already is, but..."

"Then why did you agree to this?"

She sighed. "Do you know the first thing about my son? Besides that he was a brown boy who got caught in the wrong place at the wrong time?"

I tried to keep my smile as my eyes dipped down. "Not any more than I found out at the trial. He loved baseball, and he was in that alley because he worked nights as a stock boy. It's a terrible life for a kid. They really should pass some child labor laws or something."

"It's the worst," Grace said. "I always thought I failed him, not being able to provide the life he deserved, and then I knew I failed him after he died."

"No, you didn't. It's not your fault—"

"Well, it's not his, and it seems it isn't yours, either. The trial was sure about that." She tried to steady her breathing. "Do you regret what you did to my boy?"

I bit my lip, trying not to cry. Grace wasn't doing anything to stop her own tears. "Every minute of every day. I don't do much else except think about it, truth be told. It haunts my memories, and I wake up in a cold sweat most nights after seeing him in my dreams."

She thought for a minute. "Good. That makes it a little better, at least."

"You have to believe that I didn't mean"—now the tears were flowing—"I'm so sorry I didn't see your boy."

She shook as she listened to me. "He—he was a good boy. Never made a fuss. They say boys are the devil when they grow up, but he was an angel. Always helped around the house. Never left a mess. Did his schoolwork. If his father could have seen him—maybe they'll meet up in Heaven, 'cuz he was a real good boy."

"I believe it. I mean, I have no doubt. Do you believe that?"

"It's all I have, so I have no choice. Otherwise, this is all for nothing." She reached into her purse and pulled out a picture. She slid it over to me. "I want you to have this. It's a picture of my boy when he was happy—he was always happy. Never made a fuss."

It was a picture I saw in the trial when the prosecutors tried to paint me as a monster. They brought out a smiling picture of Vincent, with curly black hair and deep, brown eyes, and made him out to be innocent. I didn't think anybody could be as innocent as they made Vincent out to be, but from what his mother told me, perhaps he was every bit the self-sacrificing child that they made him out to be.

He was no older than Xhang, and I already knew all too well what Wonderland did to kids that young. Not many could get out of Wonderland with a clean conscience, and Vincent didn't either, but he was as close as any ever came.

"You won't have to worry about me no more. I'm moving out of my place this week. Heading out into the country for a fresh start. Every block here reminds me of my boy, and I just can't—" Her words twisted inside her mouth as her tears overcame her. I reached forward and wrapped her in my arms. For a moment, it was fine, and then she realized what had happened and pulled back. "None of that, now."

It was too late, though. The media had their picture. *Disgraced cop comforts her assaulter. News at 10.*

# CHAPTER THIRTY

It was a picture-perfect moment, and Poppy must have known it because moments later, the shade closed, and darkness fell over us all once again.

"Well done, Detective!" Poppy beamed as her shoes clacked toward me. "I didn't think you had it in you, but you proved me wrong."

Grace wiped her tears away with some scratchy napkins from the metal container in front of her. "Don't ever touch me again, Detective, and let's hope our paths never cross in this life or the next."

Grace stomped off to the back room as Poppy came up to me to shake my hand. "I can't tell you how excited I am with how this all turned out."

I growled as I stood to confront her. "You got your picture, and you had your moment. You're very good at your job, Miss Poppy, but I hate your job, so if you need another photo op, get some other toady to do it."

Poppy smiled even wider as she spoke. I didn't even know a mouth could grow that big.

"But you're such a good toady, Detective, and the media simply loves you. I think you might be missing your calling in front of the camera."

I shook my head as I slid past her. "No, thank you. I'm going to go do some real work now."

The reporters lay in wait for me outside the restaurant. While Poppy protected me on the way in, there was nobody to guide me to my car through the onslaught of reporters peppering me with questions.

"Are you friends now?" one reporter shouted.

"Do you still feel shame at what you did?" another said.

"How do you live with yourself?" another yelled.

I nearly pelted them, but I knew if I did, I would be forced to do another photo op, and I just wanted to forget all of this and do my job. Every time I was out in the public eye, my job got harder and harder. Not to mention the fact that every time I picked at the festering wound that was my worst day of my life, my body nearly seized up.

I was able to keep myself together, though only just, until I pushed through them to my car and took a deep breath before turning the car on. The reporters had glommed onto my car, still screaming their questions and snapping their cameras.

"HEY!" a booming voice shouted. "Get away from the car!"

I turned to see Dormouse smiling at me. He made his way to the car and slid into the passenger's seat.

"What are you doing here?" I asked.

"I finished with Xhang and figured I would stop by and see if you were still kissing babies or doing whatever you do for the media." I smiled for a moment before he continued. "You said you had a lead, right?"

"Oh…yeah," I replied glumly.

"Then let's go. Just like old times, right?"

I sighed. "Just like old times."

I put the car in drive and started down the road, careful to avoid hitting the reporters still spread thinly around my car. That's all I needed. *Disgraced cop runs over reporter. News at 11.*

"Where are we going?" he asked as I sped through a green light to put space between the malt shop and me. "You seemed like you had something hot and spicy to check out."

"It's not much, just something Xhang said. I assume he told you about the White Queen."

"Oh yeah, and that was a big bag of bologna."

"You think he was lying?"

"I don't know if he was lying, but he definitely wasn't telling the whole truth. Don't tell me you bought what he was selling?"

"I dunno. We're supposed to check out every lead, aren't we? Isn't that our job?"

He shook his head. "No. Our job is to catch criminals."

"And clear people of crimes, too, right? I mean, I know that he's not the most trustworthy character I've ever met, but I've taken leads from people much worse than that kid that panned out."

He leaned back in his chair. "I think your radar is off, Liddell. You're chasing bunnies down rabbit holes, and no good can come of it."

His words were biting. I knew the tone well. Nearly everyone I met since the incident had the same awful tone when they spoke to me. I never thought it would come from my partner, too.

"I know you're trying to help, but you're being incredibly condescending. What happened to your car anyway?"

"I left it around the block from the malt shop. I can pick it up later."

I pulled off at a bus stop and put the car in park. "Maybe you should get it now."

"What the hell, Alice? Can't take a joke?"

"I can take a joke, but this isn't that. It's something—there's a tone in your voice, and I don't like it. I know I'm not perfect, but I'm a detective just like you."

He scoffed.

"What's that for?"

"Nothing," he said, snippy.

"No, not nothing. We have been partners as far back as I can remember. If you have something to say, then say it."

He turned toward me, anger drenched on his face. "You really want to go there?"

"Yes, let's go there. Why not?"

"Fine, but don't say I didn't warn you." He sneered. "We're not the same detective. For instance, I never killed a kid in the line of duty."

I scoffed. "Oh, that's what this is about?"

"No." I could see him trying to hold back as if a dam was about to break, and he knew it would change everything, but after a few seconds of consternation, his mouth opened again. "It's about that you should have been stripped of your badge, and yet here you are, still my partner after all these—do you know the level of harassment I've gotten since th—how much harassment my family has gotten? And yet, you walk around like it's nothing."

"Nothing?" I couldn't help but laugh. "I can barely keep it together every day. I'm a nervous wreck, and on top of that—"

He rubbed his mouth. "And on top of all that, I'm trying to protect you, like I always have, but you're making it impossible!"

"How dare—I don't need your protection."

"Oh, yes, you do. You always have, and you always will."

"You're worse than the rest of them. At least they hate me out in the open, instead of behind some façade of being a hero." I bit my lip. "Get out."

"No, we have a case."

"Get. THE FUCK. Out of my car. Right now. That wasn't a request. It was a demand."

He crossed his arms. "And if I don't?"

My eyes narrowed at him. "Then, well, you clearly believe I have no qualms killing a kid, so what do you think I would do to somebody who pissed me off worse than anybody else has in my whole life?"

"Are you threatening me?" he asked. "Unbelievable."

"Just get out."

He blew out a breath of thick, hot air and opened the door. "Fuck you, Alice. I tried to look out for you, but you're impossible."

He slammed the car door, and I sped forward around a corner and down another block so he didn't have to hear me break down and cry.

# CHAPTER THIRTY-ONE

I lost myself in tears. Dormouse was the only rock I had left, except my sister, and she didn't understand me. Dormouse did, always had. Now his truth had been revealed, and mine along with it. I was alone. *Utterly and completely alone.*

I couldn't go back to the station and find a new partner. Half the department hated me before I shot a child, and the other half loathed me now for getting special treatment.

"I need to see the doctor," I said to the receptionist at my headshrinker's office.

She smiled at me. "He's in with an appointment, and he's booked all afternoon. You are welcome to schedule with him for another day, though."

I slammed my hands on the desk. "This is an emergency."

"I understand, but—"

As she shuddered in fear, the door to the office opened, and my psychologist stepped out. "Is everything all right?"

"No," I said, my eyes still beet red. "Nothing is all right. I need to talk to you, and I need to do it now. Please."

He looked at me for a moment, mulling it over, and then held up his finger for me to wait. He disappeared into his office, and moments later, a short woman with a big purse scampered out past me, and he welcomed me into his office.

"This is highly unusual, Detective. I am making an exception for you because I can see you are in distress, but—" He cocked his head and looked down at the badge on my hip. "Wait, are you on the job right now?"

I sat down in the chair across from him. "If you can call it that. I had to—" I stopped, trying to catch myself from crying again. "It's a long story."

He bit the edge of his pencil. "It seems some time has opened up in my schedule, more than enough for a long story."

So, I told him everything about Dormouse and meeting with Vincent's mother. He sat and listened, a blank look on his face that freaked me out. He didn't speak, allowing the silence to fill the room when I took a breath. He didn't interject or comment. He didn't even move much more than a slight muscle spasm until he was sure I was done.

When I finally placed my head in my hands and took a deep breath, he tapped his pen on the pad he kept in his lap. "That is quite a lot to deal with in one day. It's not uncommon for a partner to have some resentment or jealousy after something like this. However, you are not responsible for his behavior. I hope you know that."

"No, because I think I'm the one that shot that poor kid in the face. That was me, and me alone, and I think I'm the one that forced myself back into active duty."

"You are responsible for your actions, yes, but you are not responsible for his response to them unless you intended to injure him by doing them. Did you intend to injure Detective Dormouse when you carried out either of those actions?"

"No, of course not." I sighed. "I didn't even think about him, honestly, or how it would affect his life. If he passed through my brain, I thought he would be happy to see me. I didn't think I would be a burden—not to him. I didn't think that what I did would— Maybe he's right. Maybe I am a monster."

He stroked his beard. "Interesting you use that word because monsters aren't always bad, are they? There are plenty of monsters in literature and movies and television that have done good, are there not?"

"I guess so," I replied. "There was that show about the vampire detective when I was young. I always watched it when it was on. The detective didn't seem so bad."

"The one thing about monsters is that they are misunderstood by the society they are in. A vampire wouldn't be a monster in a room full of monsters. They would be normal, but in a room full of humans, they would be a monster, and, conversely, in a room full of vampires, a human would be a monster."

I thought for a moment before nodding. "I'm not sure if I follow you completely, Doc, but I think I get your meaning. Still, I don't want to be the odd one out. I just want to be normal."

"I understand that better than you might imagine, Detective Liddell. Many of my patients claim to be monsters, but sometimes a monster is the hero we all need."

"I'm not a hero."

"Maybe, but you are misunderstood." The doctor bounced his foot on his knee. "The eyes of the world are on you now, but they will not always be. The wounds Detective Dormouse and Miss Grace have are raw now, but they will heal with time and scab over. They will never go away, but with any luck, both will move on from them, and so should you. I will not condone your actions, but you should not be held prisoner by them either. Nobody should be judged by the worst minute of their life, but by the totality of it, and you now have a chance to, over the next decades, determine whether you will be defined by your worst actions or rise above them to create something beautiful."

"It's…so hard, Doc. It's so, so hard."

"I know, and it will be for a long time, but at some point, even this will fade. My goal is to get you to a place where you aren't locked in place by your actions but can move past them in a positive direction."

"It doesn't seem possible."

"That's why you have to do the work. Unfortunately, sometimes, the only cure is time, and even then, only if you make the most of the time you have."

"Thanks, Doc."

# CHAPTER THIRTY-TWO

I couldn't say that I felt much better after leaving the psychologist, but at least I wasn't a bundle of frazzled nerves. Now, at least I wasn't crying uncontrollably and shaking like a leaf. When I approached my car, I felt capable of doing my job.

"We need to talk." A deep voice came from behind me. I knew it was Dormouse before I turned to see him.

"How did you know I was here?" I asked breathlessly.

"Doctor called the captain, who called me to tell me to get my partner in line. Aman doesn't like when one of his detectives makes a scene at a shrink's office."

"That fucking doctor. I thought everything was confidential."

Dormouse shook his head. "Not when you slam your hand on a desk and scare a poor secretary. Then, it has to be filed with the department."

I balled my fists. "I knew I shouldn't have trusted that sna—"

"It's not his fault," Dormouse said, taking a step closer.

"Whose fault is it then? Mine?"

He chuckled. "You are the one who stormed in there."

I stepped toward him. I felt the heat of his breath on my face. "I'm broken, Dormouse. You have always known that about me. This whole thing broke me more, and when I found out you weren't on my side—" I looked up at him. I could have lost myself in those big, brown eyes once, but now… "I thought you would always be on my side."

He wrapped his big, strong hands around mine. "I am on your side. I'm sorry. You just…bring out the worst in me sometimes."

"And you bring out the best in me."

There was a long moment between us, and then he reached in and kissed me, passionately and aggressively, in a way he hadn't in a long time. I went rigid for a moment, and then I remembered the grooves of his arms and fell into them. He slammed me against the car, and I wrapped my legs around him.

It had been so long since he took me into his embrace, I nearly forgot how warm he felt, and how every nook of his body fell perfectly into mine.

"Are you sure—"

I started when he came up to take a breath, but he answered by opening the back seat of my car and sliding us both inside. Things were not always well with Dormouse and his wife, and in those days, he found comfort in my bed, but those days were a long time ago, back before their second child.

I had been with a lot of men since Dormouse, but there was never one that made me feel as safe when he took control of me. He had barely pulled off my jeans before he was inside me, and all the bitterness and hatred I felt for myself, all my sadness, was replaced with the rush of ecstasy and exhilaration as he penetrated me again and again. I climaxed once and then again before we both came together, and he pulled me close, his hot breath against my heaving breast.

In the heat of the moment, I forgot we were parked in a lot underneath a medical building, and as I rolled off him, the thought of somebody seeing us raised the exhilaration and gave me a jolt of joy. I was always his dirty little secret, and now, it was out in the open.

"That was…different," I said, pulling my pants back on. "I thought we weren't doing that anymore.

"I—" He turned away from me. "I don't know what came over me. You have no idea how hard the last few months have been on me, trying to protect your reputation while my family—I don't regret what I said to you, but I do regret how I said it."

"You still think I should be kicked off the force?"

"Not off—I think you need more time for the heat to die down and for you to get your mind right. You have no idea how many people are rooting against you out there, and I can't protect you against them. Every time I try, they come for my family and remind me I'm a black man in a predominantly white department."

I buttoned up my pants. "I'm not going to hide, Dormouse. I'm not going to get another job. I'm not going to be run off from the one thing I love in this whole world—" I looked over at him and saw his face contort. "Not you, the job. I've wanted to be a NARCO since I was a kid, and yeah, it's not what I thought it would be, but it's the only thing I'm good at. Sitting at home, it drove me crazy. I know I did something terrible, but I can't make up for it by lounging on the couch. I can only make up for it out on the streets, taking down the people who caused me to—well, you know."

"And what if you can't make up for it?" Dormouse asked.

"I can't think like that, or I'd shoot myself in the head." I looked over at him. "I need you on my side, whether this was a one-time thing or not. It doesn't have to get messy between us, but I need you to have my back out there and at the precinct."

"I'll have your back, even if I don't agree with you, but Alice, regardless of this, my family is what I care about most of all. They come first, then you, then the department. If you do anything to put them in danger—"

"I won't," I piped in quickly. "I swear to that."

"I believe you, but if you do, I won't hesitate to protect them with everything in my being."

"Fair," I replied. "Now, can we please go do our jobs?"

# CHAPTER THIRTY-THREE

I knew it was cliché to sleep with your partner, especially as a female cop, but when Dormouse and I started working together, we fell into a rhythm. We worked too late into the night, then grabbed drinks and fell asleep exhausted until the following day. Eventually, proximity and libidos got the best of us, and convenience won out over reason and logic. He would have a bad day, or I would have a bad day, and it became a logical next step in our relationship. Nobody got hurt, and we both got our rocks off.

It was good, too, way too good when I was with him. When he met Charlotte, I moved on to other men, but when they had problems and he needed a shoulder to cry on, I was there, and then he was in my bed. There was a lot of guilt at first, but that didn't stop it from happening again and again and again until he decided he couldn't do it anymore, and I respected that.

I had my own string of flames, but none of them really understood the job or what it took from me, so they never lasted. I didn't hold a torch for Dormouse, but he was always there and convenient. It was easy to lay my problems onto him and then use him as the standard by which I judged all men. When put up against my partner, everyone else was found wanting.

Not that Dormouse was perfect, of course. After all, he had cheated on his wife with me, repeatedly, but he was a known commodity. I already accepted him, warts and all. Compared to a new man, there was no comparison. My sister thought I was holding him up to others to have a reason to keep an invisible barrier around myself, and I agreed. He barricaded me from having to get too close to anyone.

Maybe that was why it broke me so much when he betrayed me, because not only did I think I lost my partner, but also my shield against everything else. Or maybe it was because that was just a shitty thing to do to somebody you cared about.

"Where are we going?" Dormouse asked as we drove through the south side of Wonderland. I turned into a neighborhood filled with row houses.

"Xhang told you he was dealing Rabbit, right?"

Dormouse nodded. "Yup, for the White Queen. Have you ever heard of her before?"

I shook my head. "Not until today. He gave me the name of his dealer but swore me to secrecy. I agreed, but I guess since you've been inside me today, I can trust you with the whole truth." I looked up to the crumbling row house across the street. It was nothing like the apartment in Antieque. However, most dealers didn't live in fancy digs. That was the fallacy, the lie everyone needed to believe to sign up for the dangerous life, the promise of fast cash.

"And this is his connection's house?"

I nodded. "She's employed by the White Queen."

"We should be careful, then."

"I'm always careful." I opened the door. "Except when I'm not."

The paint was chipping off the side of the house, and the porch beams were not straight vertical, making the whole structure look like it was going to fall at any moment or with the slightest knock on the door.

"Go around back, just in case," I said to Dormouse. He nodded and disappeared around the edge of the structure two houses down. The other houses connected to the drug dealer's weren't the model of pristine, but none were quite as dilapidated as the one whose stairs creaked as I stepped up on them.

I gently rapped on the door, trying my best to convey that I wasn't a police officer. If there was a criminal inside, I didn't want to spook them. I didn't hear anything for a moment, but then footsteps hopped onto the roof above me and rushed to the edge of the porch, where somebody in a hoodie leaped onto a tree across from the house and shimmied down to the ground.

"FREEZE!" I shouted, pulling my weapon. It shook in my hands as I tried to level it at the woman. "I don't want to hurt you."

The hooded figure turned to me for a moment, smiled, and then took off down the street. I jumped down the stairs to chase after her, but she was fast. Really fast. I pulled my gun up to shoot, but when I leveled my legs and stood straight, my finger couldn't pull the trigger. All I saw was Vincent's smiling face, dripping blood, and my confidence disappeared.

I holstered the gun and took off running once again. "Dormouse! Help!"

I took off across the street to give chase, but the culprit hopped onto a motorcycle and gunned it down the street, turned the corner, and disappeared from sight.

# CHAPTER THIRTY-FOUR

*It was a total loss.*

Not only did we tip off the White Queen that we're onto her, but there was nothing useful in the house that could lead us in the right direction. A small fire burned in the metal trash can at the top of the stairs, filled with charred papers and the like, but otherwise, it was like a ghost lived there. Only the bare essentials were sprinkled around the house, and they were in such disrepair and filled with mold that it was hard to believe anybody could remain that way for long after sitting on them.

"It's okay, Liddell," Dormouse said as he met me outside the house. I spent the last hour canvassing the neighborhood, only to learn that the perp we were waiting for moved in two months ago, blared trap music late into the night, and was never seen during the day. Maybe she really was a ghost.

"It's not okay," I replied. "I wasn't even suppo—" I caught myself before telling him that I wasn't supposed to tell him anything. "I told the kid that I couldn't put the heat on him, but I have a hard time believing this won't blow back at him somehow."

"Did you grow a heart, Alice? You don't normally bond to your arrests."

He was right, and it wasn't like I bonded to Xhang, but there was the ticking time bomb of Caterpillar to deal with, and that wild card kept me on my toes.

"He's a kid, man," I said, trying to mask my fear. "And since…well, I have a thing about kids now, okay? So, sue me."

Dormouse decided that the best course of action was heading down to the company records office to find the owner of the property. I couldn't deny that idea, but I found it hard to believe the White Queen would leave a paper trail. Criminals were usually more intelligent than that, at least by the time they reached kingpin status.

"Good afternoon, Francisco," Dormouse said, walking in through the door. He was on a first-name basis with most people in City Hall, while I tried my hardest to avoid them. "Que pasa?"

Francisco gritted through his smile as he listened to Dormouse's terrible accent. "Going well, Dormouse, and you?"

"I can complain, but I won't." He smiled brightly. "Do you think you can pull up a house deed for me? I didn't find anything searching online."

Francisco nodded and took the paper from Dormouse's hand before disappearing into the stacks of records behind him. We long ago moved to keeping most of our records digitally, but the important stuff was still backed up in paper, including land sale records. Somebody could wipe a hard drive or steal a file, but few could do both, at least before somebody found out.

"That's weird," Francisco said, scratching his head as he came forward with a slender file. "That house is over a hundred years old, but it looks like it's never been sold after its original owner."

"Why is that weird?" I asked, even though Francisco's eyes found Dormouse first.

"Well, most people don't live to be over a hundred years old, and they certainly don't buy houses as newborns. Even if this couple bought their house at the young age of twenty, they would have to be a hundred and twenty, and somebody that old, a couple no less, would be news. If they died, the title would have transferred to somewhere, either next of kin, or a bank at the very least, and if none of that happened, we would have repossessed it for not paying property taxes. This is very weird. Of course, weird things did happen during the Red Queen's reign. We're still picking up the pieces."

"Thanks, Francisco," Dormouse said, taking the file.

He was right, too. When we returned to the station, I looked up the death records for the owners of the house, Meryl and Edgar Filch, and sure enough, Meryl died twenty-seven years ago, during the tail end of the Red Queen's reign, and Edgar died eleven years later. He never remarried and only had one relation, a nephew who was in his sixties, living in a suburb outside of the city.

"This is really weird," Dormouse said. "Francisco was right. I'm not completely sure what we are looking at."

"Let's have forensics pull up a list of people who died without kin in the last decade and see if we can find a pattern in their housing records."

"I'll make the call." His phone beeped, and he looked down at it. "Damn, it's late already. Can you do it, actually? I have to get home to coach my daughter's tee ball team."

I tried to hide the pain in my voice. I didn't pine for Dormouse, but I did like his wife. She was kind and forgiving, and we completely took advantage of that by sleeping with each other.

"Of course," I replied. "Go be with your family."

It wasn't like I had one of my own, so I was happy to do the grunt work for him. He would do the same for me if the situation was reversed. Or at least, I hoped he would. He already treated me like trash today, so maybe he wouldn't. Maybe I should tell him to go fuck himself, but he was the only string remaining of my sanity, so instead, I chose to hang on, even if it was stupid to do so. Or maybe it was time to find another string.

# CHAPTER THIRTY-FIVE

I hadn't been out to the suburbs in years. My sister always invited me for dinner, which happened every night at seven like boring clockwork, but I never made it out. I always told her I would come the next day, next week, or next year, but it never happened. It wasn't that I didn't love them. It was just that I couldn't stand the banality of their existence.

No, maybe that wasn't it, either. Maybe it was that I liked my life, or at least I thought I liked my life, and seeing her perfect family ground my gears down. However, it just so happened that by the time I finished with forensics, it was 5:30 p.m., with just enough time to fight traffic to my sister's house before dinnertime. After everything I'd been through, boring banality sounded wonderful.

I decided not to tell her I was coming, mostly because I couldn't take it if she told me she was busy. Every hour I teetered closer to the break of another crack in my psyche. On top of that, another thought started to crack through the top of my brain—how everything was simple in Wonderland.

Not the Wonderland I knew, but the one I found when I was on Rabbit. I had been fighting the niggling thought for days, but when I was high on Rabbit, nothing else mattered. My doctors were ham sandwiches, and my nurses were purple flamingos, and nothing made sense, but everything did. There were no duplicitous, cheating partners or holes in the pits of your stomach. You didn't watch the world stare at you with punitive hatred like you had never done anything good with your life, and you never would.

No, in the haze of Rabbit, you didn't have to worry about any of that. You got to live in blissful ignorance, willful ignorance, brought on by the best drug trip of your life. The more shit that piled on top of my back, the more the thought of Wonderland, the Wonderland from the Red Queen's time, made a whole lot of sense.

It made me understand my father, and I hated that about myself. The one thing I always knew, unequivocally, about my father was that he was a piece of garbage for getting strung out on Rabbit, but now everything was flipped on its head. I truly was my father's daughter.

I arrived at my sister's house with ten minutes to spare after fighting traffic. There were times when the drive took less than thirty minutes, but not during rush hour when everyone was trying to flee the city.

My hand shook as I knocked on the door to the house. My sister lived in a palace compared to my shithole of an apartment. She had the blue house with the white-washed shutters and the white picket fence where her children could play with their shaggy dog. It was the kind of life I sometimes wished I wanted to have, but I simply couldn't do it.

"Hang on, honey!" Dinah shouted from the other side of the door. "I'll bet it's a pack—" Her body froze when she saw me. "Alice?"

I smiled at her. "Hi, sis. I was hoping maybe I could cash in on that long overdue dinner invitation."

She looked stunned for a moment and then smiled brightly. "Of course, you can! Josh, Evie, and Chaz will be pleased as punch to see you."

Nobody had been pleased to see me for a long time, so I doubted her claim, but then the two cutest children in the whole world rushed out of the kitchen and into my arms.

They smelled of cinnamon and cardamom and just a little bit like butt.

"Auntie Alice!" Their voices were filled with joy. They each pulled me in different directions. "Come see my trains!" little Chaz said, while Evie screamed, "Watch me play the guitar," as she dragged me in the other direction.

"Children," Dinah said in her best "mom voice." "Let's eat, and then I'm sure Alice will play with both of you, won't you?"

I nodded. "Of course. That's why I'm here."

"Yay!" they both screamed as they ran back to the kitchen. I heard them pull out their seats in the dining room as Dinah walked up to me.

"You must be doing pretty shitty if you came here." She handed me a full glass of wine. "Here."

I chuckled to her. "You don't know the half of it."

"Well, I know quite a bit, and it's all bad, so the thought there might be more fills me with dread." She wrapped her arm around me. "Let's get a home-cooked meal in you, and then once I put the kids to bed, you can tell me all about it."

I let out a deep sigh. "That sounds nice."

And for the first time in all my trips to her house, I really, honestly meant it.

# CHAPTER THIRTY-SIX

I spent an hour playing with Chaz and Evie, letting them pull me back and forth across the house as they showed me everything from their rooms to their toys to their schoolwork before they tired themselves out and crashed.

I took my wine outside into the cool night air and listened to the crickets chirp as I stared up into the stars.

"It's peaceful, right?" Josh said, walking outside with a blanket. "I thought you could use this. It gets chilly at night, and I know you're a tough city girl who would never ask." He placed the blanket on the table next to me and patted it. "So I'll leave it here, in case."

I was too proud to take it for a second, but I quickly recanted and wrapped myself in it as the chill crawled up my spine. "Thanks."

"It's good to see you. I'm glad you made it out tonight."

I smiled. "The kids have gotten so big. Last time I saw them, Evie was barely talking, and Josh was into…what was it? Spiders?"

"Insects, including spiders."

"Even though they are arachnids?"

"He wasn't picky back then." Josh looked up at the stars. "Now he's into big trucks. They're remodeling a house down the block, and he makes me walk him down there every day to look at the dump trucks."

"Sounds exhausting."

He nodded. "Yeah, but in a good way. You know, looking at them, it's hard to get caught up with the bullshit of the day."

I took a sip of wine. "Doesn't it freak you out more when things go wrong, though, since you have them to take care of too?"

He chuckled. "Sometimes it gets to be a lot, but for the most part, we have our needs covered, and both our jobs are stable."

"Sounds terrible."

"For you, but I'm not like you. I don't need my job to be fulfilling or even fun. I get that from them." He pointed up to the lights in the rooms upstairs, where I could make out the shadow of Dinah finishing tucking the kids into bed. "I do it all for them, and that's enough."

"I used to think that was the worst thing in the world." I rimmed my finger around the outside of the glass, producing a low moan from it. "But after the last couple of weeks, maybe that's not so bad."

The lights went off upstairs, and it caught Josh's eye before he turned back to me. "Looks like the kids are down for the night. Dinah will be down soon, and she's a better listener than me. Night, Alice."

Josh wasn't one for comforting talk either, and when he was done with a conversation, he simply left it, even if I had more to say. For many years it was disturbing, and I thought it rude, but now I admired it. Imagine having the confidence to turn away from somebody when you had nothing interesting left to say.

He turned back to the house, and I wanted to say more but let him go. I wasn't one to reach out, and we weren't the type to say things like "I love you" to each other. It was hard enough for me to say it to Dinah, and even then, I barely had the energy.

I sat outside, under my blanket, for another five minutes, trying to keep the sad thoughts at bay, before Dinah walked out and rushed to the blanket. "Give me some of that."

She slid under the blanket and curled up in the chair next to me with her own glass of wine. I laid my head on her shoulder as we looked up at the stars.

"I always forget how many more stars there are out here."

She sipped her wine before laying her head on mine. "It's one of the things I love most about this place. I told you there was a beauty to it. You just don't want to see it."

I took a sip of wine. "I like what I like."

"You like what you know, and what you know is that dirty, grungy city, but I'm telling you from experience, this is better."

My back began to heave as I cried into her shoulder. She placed her wine down and grabbed mine to do the same before wrapping me in her arms. She let me cry for a long time, in the dark of the night, as the crickets chirped. She whispered sweet words and told me it would all be okay as she rubbed my back. When I finally calmed a bit, she rocked back and forth to soothe me like I was a little baby until, finally, I stopped and took a deep breath.

"Feel better?" she asked.

I wanted to lie, but instead, the truth vomited from my mouth. "No, not even a little bit. This last—it's been horrible, Dinah. I don't know what to do."

She listened as I told her everything, except for my contract with Caterpillar. From the moment she helped bathe me to the dalliance with Dormouse, to the seething hatred of my fellow officers, and everything in between. When I was done, I felt empty, numb, and bereft of any feeling. It was actually nice, in its way, to feel nothing instead of everything, especially when that 'everything' was bad.

When I was done venting, Dinah picked up her glass and took a big sip. I hadn't realized she finished most of it as I was talking, but my life would lead even the strongest person in the world to drink.

"That's pretty fucked," Dinah said. "I'm not going to lie. I knew it was pretty fucked, but that is extremely fucked."

I smiled. "You don't curse."

"Which tells you how bad it is for you if I can't think of any other words." She rubbed the dryness off the sides of her mouth. "Plus, you know me. I don't curse until I do, and then I can't fucking turn it off, just like that."

"What do I do?"

"I don't know." She shrugged. "I'm not a psychologist."

"I have a psychologist. He sucks."

"Then you need a better one, and it's not gonna be me. If you had a skinned knee or didn't know how to add fractions together, then I might be helpful, but this is heavy stuff you are dealing with, and I have no fucking idea how to pull you out of it." She took another sip. "You remember what happened when shit got too bad for me?"

"Yeah, you fled."

She finished her glass. "It's what I do best."

"But you built a life here. I don't see you fleeing now."

She placed her glass down. "I think about it sometimes, honestly. Don't tell Josh, but I really fucking do when things pile up. But he has a way of making it all better and never freaking out about it. It puts me at ease."

"So, I need a Josh."

She smiled. "Don't you dare. I know how you feel about married men."

"I would never—"

"I know, that was a bad joke." She sighed. "I think you should definitely never sleep with your partner again."

"I say that every time, but then—well, it's a stressful job, and this is a stressful time."

"Then go to the bar and pick up a rando."

"Done that, too. It's not the same as somebody who knows you."

"Fuck, Alice." She took the glass out of my hand and took a sip. "You are a mess."

I yanked the glass out of her hand. "I know it. I'm not proud of any of this shit."

"And yet you keep digging yourself a hole." She leaned forward. "Maybe you need to come out here, not forever, but until things blow over. I know the kids would love to have you, and we have that spare bedroom in the basement. It would be like your own private space."

"God, has it really gotten that bad?"

"You're goddamn right it has," she said. "I know you won't take it because you think you can get out of a hole by continuing to dig, but the offer is open."

"Thanks." I leaned my head against her shoulder. "I'm not staying for long, but can I stay here tonight? I don't think I'm okay to drive."

"Of course," she said as I finished my drink. "You can stay here as long as you would like. Come on. I'll show you to your room."

# CHAPTER THIRTY-SEVEN

It took me a while to fall asleep without the white noise of the city. I found, after so many years, that the cars and the sirens and the murmurs of the street soothed me, but once I finally found sleep, I stayed asleep undisturbed until the following morning, when I was jolted from bed by a pair of small feet jostling me up and down.

My eyes popped open in a start to see Evie leaping up and down on my bed, laughing and smiling.

"It's morning!" she shouted when she saw my eyes were open. "It's morning, it's morning, it's moooooorning!"

"Evie!" Dinah shouted. "Get down from there. I'm so sorry, Alice. I told her you were here, then turned around, and she was gone."

I yawned as she picked her child up. "It's okay. It's fine. What time is it?"

"Almost seven. It's the witching hour trying to get them ready for school."

"I'll get up and help you."

"It's okay; you're a guest. You don't have to."

I pushed myself up to my elbows. "No, no. It's fine. I'm not a guest. I'm your sister."

Some people had extensive morning routines, stretches and meditation, and such, but my morning routine was to get out of bed and put on clothes, maybe grab a shower if I was lucky, before heading to the station. I looked at my phone to see a half dozen messages from Dormouse, wondering where I was, and a missed call from the forensics lab.

Any other day I would have rushed back to the office, but I had no interest in fighting traffic, and I knew Dormouse could handle it without me. It wasn't like the world would burn down before I got to the office, and if it did, it would prove I was as important as I thought I was to the world. It was a win-win.

I went to the bathroom, where I found a note from Dinah taped to a new toothbrush. I splashed water on my face and brushed my teeth. When I got back to my room, she had left out a new black T-shirt for me and a pair of underwear.

"I left clothes for you!" she shouted from downstairs. "They're from the last time you stayed here. I hope you didn't get fat in the last few years."

I laughed. "If anything, I got thinner. Stress does that to you."

"I have breakfast for you down here. Hurry up if you want to help take them to school."

"I just won't shower!" I shouted back.

"No, please. You stink. Shower."

It was the kind of thing only a sister could say without it sounding like an insult. She really was looking out for me, and one sniff of my pits proved her point. She was right. I needed a shower. It always took a while for the shower to get hot in her house. The water heater was stretched to the limit, so I undressed while I waited, looking at myself in the mirror when I was done.

I lost definition in my arms over the months since the incident, and you could see my ribs. I never ate much, but these days I wasn't hungry for anything, even the greasy burgers and pizza I used to gulp down while on the job. I didn't even eat at the diner with Xhang, except for stealing a few of his fries. Dinner last night was the first full meal I could remember.

I didn't care for showers, so I didn't stay in long. Just long enough to let the water fall down my back and rub myself clean. The clothes were baggy on me, but no more so than anything in my closet. I should buy new ones, but I always intended to get back to the gym and bulk back up, so I put it off. Nothing worse than getting new clothes and then growing out of them a month later.

No, that's not true. So many things were worse, and I had dealt with most of them in the recent past.

The kids were stuffing their faces with waffles and fruit when I entered the kitchen, and Dinah pushed a plate piled high with them over to me before turning to Chaz.

"Did you finish your homework?" He kicked his feet under his chair before rolling his eyes. "Don't give me that look. You know what Mrs. Hansen will say if you don't bring it in again."

"Yes, Moooooom," he said.

"Do I need to check it?" she asked. "Because if I get another call—"

"Mom, I did it. God." To have that kind of angst over nothing once again and to feel bitterness at a mother's love.

"Children are so great at this age." Dinah gave a quick, false smile to me before turning to Evie. "And what about you, Miss Thing? Did you bring your book for show and tell?"

She nodded. "I did! *The Good Caterpillar*. It's my favorite." She turned to me. "Maybe you can read it to me tonight."

My stomach dropped because I knew I was headed back soon. "Maybe. Let's play that one by ear, okay?"

"Okay!" Evie said. She still didn't understand that maybe almost always meant no.

After breakfast, I helped them stuff into the car and drove them to school. They were both in elementary school, with Chaz in fifth grade and Evie in first. Their backpacks were half the size of them, and they looked comical as Dinah kissed them goodbye and walked them to the door.

"You do this every morning?" I said. "Before work? Isn't that a lot?"

She shrugged as we walked back to the car. "They are only this age once, and I don't plan on having another one, so I do it, even though it's hard."

"I guess I understand that. I do plenty of things I don't like because of reasons way stupider than that."

We got back to the car and turned the ignition. "I'm assuming I will be dropping you back off at your car."

I nodded. "I appreciate the offer, but there are some things I have to wrap up in the city before I even consider leaving."

"It's not a good place, Alice. I know you think it's amazing, or whatever, but there are so many other places you could do good that would appreciate you. Hell, you don't even have to be a cop. I can put in a word for you at the—"

I put up my hand. "I appreciate that, Dinah. I really do, but I'm a cop through and through. It's what I'm good at, and it's in my blood." My phone vibrated. It was Dormouse. "I need to get this."

"Where the Hell are you?" Dormouse said. "I've been calling all night."

"I'm at my sister's house. I pulled three twelve-hour shifts in a row and decided to come in late today. Don't get so twi—"

"You need to get in here as quickly as possible. The captain is having a conniption."

"What's happening?"

"Xhang. The kid we were supposed to be protecting…he's dead."

"Oh no."

My heart raced as my phone buzzed again. I looked down to see a message from Caterpillar, and my stomach dropped to my shoes. *I need to see you. Now.*

# CHAPTER THIRTY-EIGHT

It was hard to know which fire to put out first, but since Caterpillar held my future in his precious little hands, and Aman was on his payroll, I thought it best to see him first. He was not in the seat at the back of the club when I entered. Instead, he paced the room, which was unusually empty for the time of day.

"There yhou ahre!" he shouted. "Yhou were suppoooosed to make my lhife easier, not harder."

"I'm really sorry. I had no idea that—it's no excuse, but I thought that the fact you own half the police department meant they could protect one little kid."

"Whell, it seeeems yhou were mistaken, and now I have people qhestioning my ahbility to prothect them, dhon't I? Dho yhou know what happens when criminals think yhou whent sofht?" I started to nod, but it didn't matter. He was running through with his thought no matter what I did. "They come fhor yhou, and then people die. Their people, our people, my people. Do yhou whant the streets to run rhed whith blood?"

I shook my head. "No, I don't want that at all."

"Then I suggest yhou fhind Yin and the person who killed little Xhang, and dho it quickly." He stormed toward me. "What ahre you still dhoing here?"

I didn't wait another moment before turning on my heels and running out of the club. Silly me to think I could have one night to recover before the world collapsed around me. That was too much to ask, surely, and now I didn't even have time to panic about it because if I didn't fix all this quickly, the world would quite literally burn.

The whole of Wonderland sat upon a powder keg for too long, and all it needed was one person to light the match before it exploded, taking the gods only knew how many people along with it.

I pulled every trick I knew with my car to get to the station in record time. I usually didn't like swerving between people or running through lights unless I was chasing down somebody, but desperate times called for desperate actions.

The station was alight with activity when I burst through the doors, but everyone had a moment to turn and sneer at me. It wasn't clear if this was my usual animosity or something graver, but my nerves had been steeled by my anxiety, and I locked myself off from feeling anything about their anger until after I fixed this. I would allow myself to collapse into a mental breakdown soon, but not yet. Now, we had work to do.

"Goddamn it, Liddell!" Aman shouted when the door opened to the bullpen. "You really shit the bed on this one!"

"Me?" I shouted. "I left Xhang in your care, and now he's dead. How is this my fault?"

He didn't answer. He just turned into his office. "Just fix it!"

That was like him, to saddle me with the responsibility of fixing his mistake. I rushed over to Dormouse's desk to hear him deep in conversation with somebody. When he saw me, he looked grimly at me. "I have to call you back."

"Who was that?"

He grabbed his coat. "The coroner. Come on. They've finished Xhang's autopsy."

"How did he die?" I asked.

"Throat was slit in his cell. The cameras had been turned off, and there's no log of anybody going in or out except for the normal patrol, and their keycards hadn't been swiped for a half-hour before or after the incident. We're at a loss." He spun to me. "Where were you last night? I thought you were handling this?"

"I called forensics, and then I went to my sister's. I'm allowed a life, too. Just because you think you can dump everything on me because I don't have a wife and kids doesn't mean I am a robot. I deserve some off time, too."

He sighed. "You're right; you do. We're all a little on edge."

"Well, don't take it out on me. I'm not the enemy here."

"I never said you were."

I turned to the elevator. "Your tone said it all. Let's fix this."

The morgue was on the lowest floor, below even the parking garage, where it was naturally cool. Most people hated the morgue, but I didn't mind it. The smell was odd, ascorbic, and sterile from all the cleaning products, but also with the distinct smell of dead bodies mixed in. However, just because I didn't mind it didn't mean I liked it, either. There was a reason I didn't go into homicide. Dead bodies freaked me out, and children even more so than others.

"As you can see," the coroner said, "there is a clean line across the neck. However, while I first believed this to be a knife, I now think somebody came up behind him and used a garrote or a piano wire to do the job."

"Shit," I said. "You can smuggle that in a pair of pants completely inconspicuously. Any signs of a struggle? Skin under the fingernails or anything we can use to get DNA?"

He shook his head. "Not that I can find. No bruises either, which means there wasn't much of a struggle, at least until the deed was too far along to fight back. There is something interesting, though."

"What's that?" I asked.

"Well, with a child this size, you would assume he would be pulled up because the assailant would be bigger than him. However, the reason we originally thought it was a knife was that the wound was straight across, indicating they were roughly the same size."

"And Xhang wasn't that tall," I said.

"No, he wasn't."

I looked down at poor Xhang. Yes, he was a drug dealer, but he was only a child. Who could have done this to somebody so young and full of life? Whoever did this was a monster.

# CHAPTER THIRTY-NINE

The morgue was on the same level as the forensics department, as they shared a lot of information between them. While I didn't spend much time in the morgue, I was in the forensics department multiple times a week.

"N'baka," I shouted to the tech at a computer at the front of the department. There weren't any rules about transitioning in the department, but most people chose to retain their human complexion. N'baka, however, was in the process of sprouting beautiful pink features to become a flamingo, and combined with his ebony black skin, it looked absolutely breathtaking.

Behind him were a dozen other computers, along with everything from beakers to centrifuges to things I couldn't name or remember when they told me about it.

"Did you find something for me?"

He pushed up his thick glasses. "There you are, Detective Liddell. I assumed I would see you today, even though I sent you a detailed report on my results."

"You know I never check my email, and I have no interest in reading your dry writing, N'baka."

"Why are we here?" Dormouse asked. "We need to get to the holding cell and check for clues."

"You can go if you want, but I doubt you'll find anything there. I think the secret is in the list of properties we asked N'baka to gather."

"You think the White Queen killed Xhang?" Dormouse asked.

"It's my best bet and the only person who would have the balls to infiltrate a police station."

"What about Caterpillar?"

I smirked. "We both know Caterpillar owns half this department. If he wanted Xhang, he wouldn't have made such a show about it. He would have had one of his lackeys take him to his lair." *Like me.* "Besides, why would Caterpillar want to kill a kid?"

He shrugged. "I dunno."

"I know it's a long shot, but if these leads can help us track down the White Queen, then we can ask her before this whole situation implodes on us." I turned to N'baka. "Please tell me you have something."

"Well, I appreciate your faith in me as always, Detective," N'baka said. "You're not wrong, of course, to trust in my abilities. I spent the evening tracking down all the properties you requested, and it seems like they all had a similar problem as the one in city hall. A dozen properties have literally fallen off the books in the past decade, with no deed or proof of ownership claims."

"And you didn't tell anyone, did you?"

N'baka shook his head. "As per your request, the only two people who know are you and me, along with, I suppose, Dormouse here since you brought him with you."

"Are you thinking these could be safe houses for the White Queen?" Dormouse asked, suddenly very interested in our conversation.

N'baka held up his hands. "I'm not making any such claims. I only process information and give the reports. Synthesizing that information is far above my pay grade."

"Can you print these out?"

N'baka sighed. "Yes, I mean, I sent them to your email to save trees, but I can print them, too, you old-school neophyte."

"While you're doing that," I looked up at Dormouse, "I believe you wanted to visit the cells?"

The cells were one floor up from forensics, still below the parking garage. If somebody wanted to sneak in, they would have to get into the garage with a keycard, enter, and go down one flight, and then swipe another keycard to get into the holding cells, and then have a key to the cells to open the door to Xhang and kill him.

"Here it is," the uniform told us as he led us into the cell. "It's the damnedest thing."

"That's an understatement," I said. "How many people have access to this cell?"

He scratched his head. "I mean, quite a few, but you would have to get buzzed in and then have a—"

I held up my hand. "I know how it works. And you didn't see anything out of the ordinary on your shift?"

"You mean besides the dead guy?" He smiled, but when he saw I wasn't amused, he stopped. "Nothing other than that, ma'am."

I turned my attention to Dormouse, who was inside the cell. "What do you see?"

He shrugged. "Not much, unfortunately. The mattress isn't even kicked over, meaning this was all over quickly. Still, there should be blood or something, though, but it's like this scene was wiped down, too."

"Like somebody cleaned up after themselves?"

He nodded. "The feed was clean for an hour—" He thought for a second before turning to the uniformed officer. "Hey, how often do you do sweeps?"

"Every hour on the hour."

"And when did the feed go out?" Dormouse said.

"I don't know. I haven't seen the tapes or anything."

Dormouse stroked his chin as he looked up at the cameras. "We need to see those tapes."

We took the elevator up to security on the third floor, far from the cells. A pudgy woman in a button-up white shirt that wasn't doing her any favors sat in front of a security bank.

"I don't know what you expect to find from just black tape, but here you go."

She pulled up the feed that went black, along with all the other feeds that were going that night on every television in the bank. Dormouse leaned in. "Just rewind it until right before the feed cuts." She sighed and did what she was told, rewinding all the tapes at the same time.

"There!" He pointed to the black feed, and sure enough, seconds before it cut, a guard had made a patrol. "I'll be damned."

"Now, move it to the right when the feed resumed." She did as she was told, and when the feed came back, within a few seconds, a guard came in to find Xhang's dead body. "They literally planned this to happen between sweeps. That's too much of a coincidence not to matter. Who was working this station that night?"

"Wait!" I shouted. "Look at this."

I looked up at one of the other televisions that rewound with the black feed. It showed a young child being led into the station by somebody. It just so happened that in that moment, they looked back at the screen, and I recognized them.

*Yin.*

# CHAPTER FORTY

"Do you see this, Dormouse?" I asked, pointing to the camera that showed the missing child. "That's the kid we're looking for. That's Yin."

Dormouse squinted at the monitor. "What's he doing in the police station?"

I thought for a moment, trying to put the pieces together. "I have a theory, but it's a wild guess."

"Better than I have. Let's hear it."

I rubbed my forehead, trying to fight off the headache behind my eyes. "Okay, if I had to guess, then I would think that Yin was on the run from Cate—for killing Chu." That much I already knew from Xhang's confession at the abandoned warehouse. "He probably went to the White Queen asking for sanctuary and was told he could only have it if he made a show of loyalty."

"And that loyalty meant killing his friend? That's cold."

"It's also tying up loose ends. Xhang was the only person besides Chu who knew about his dealer. My bet is the White Queen isn't ready to make a flashy entrance, so she wanted to silence anybody that knew about her outside of her close circle."

"And having Xhang in police custody meant he could tattle."

The pieces started making sense the more I thought about them. There was no way the White Queen would want her business known, and it would be too risky to use one of her men to infiltrate the police station. She might as well use a disposable kid, knowing if he was found out, nobody would miss him.

"Considering how many people on this payroll are dirty, that would get back to somebody and lead to a turf war she wasn't ready for…yet."

Dormouse nodded. "We need to find Yin quickly before he disappears."

"Let's go back to N'baka and get that list."

Our best lead was the list of houses that were off the books. If they were a list of the White Queen's safe houses around the city, she probably had Yin hiding out in one of them after the murder, waiting for the heat to die down so she could sneak him out of the city. Poor kid, having to make the choice between death and murder. Yes, he was a criminal, but what choice did he have, growing up in Crash Town? Dealing drugs didn't make somebody a murderer, and even Chu's death might have been an accident, but Xhang's death was premeditated.

N'baka had our printout ready when we arrived back in forensics. I asked him to print two more copies, and I handed one to Dormouse as we started up the elevator. "I'm going to try and get some backup from the captain, but we can't wait to start checking these houses. Do not enter one without me. Just start at the front of the list and move back. I'll join you when I can."

"Be careful."

"Are you kidding? You have the dangerous part of this."

"You have to convince the captain to use department resources on your harebrained idea, so I don't know if I agree with you. I'd much rather be me than you."

The captain was in with one of the lieutenants when I arrived at his office and knocked. "I need to talk to you."

"I'm in a meeting, and it's more important than—"

"It's about Xhang's killer, but I can come back."

"Wait!" Aman snarled at me. "Get out, Lieutenant. We need the room." After the lieutenant left, I closed the door and locked it, drawing the blinds when I did. "Why the secrecy?"

"I need you to find people loyal to Caterpillar on your staff. I know you're on his take, and you must know who else is, too."

"How did you—" He squinted at me. "Wait? You? I thought you were squeaky clean."

"I'm surprised Caterpillar didn't tell you yet. Maybe he wasn't sure if he would hang me out to dry, but whatever, yes, I am on the take, and he told me this morning that if I don't find Yin, he's going to raze this city to the ground until he finds him and shows he can protect his people, and that there are consequences for coming for them. I think Yin killed Xhang, and he's hiding out at one of these houses around the city."

I slammed a copy of the houses on Aman's desk.

"This is a mess." Aman bit his lip. "You're asking me to put a hit on the kid."

I shook my head. "No, I just need you to help me find him." I slid the papers toward him. "We tracked down twelve houses we think the White Queen is using to stash her people. I believe Yin is being held in one of these. We can check them one at a time, but it would be way better if we could coordinate a strike on all of them at once, before they can sneak Yin out of the area."

"That's even worse. You're asking me to use our resources in a blatant attempt to align with the Caterpillar's interest. I have strict orders from him not to make our interference too obvious, and there's nothing to warrant a strike of this type, except for your gut, and information we couldn't possibly have unless we were on the take."

He wasn't going to help me. "If he gets away, it's both of our asses."

"No, just yours, and you're a risk I'm willing to take."

"Can you at least put an APB out on somebody? Surveillance can show you the image we pulled earlier of Yin, and watch out, because if my hunch is right, then somebody in this department snuck him in to kill Xhang, which means one of your men is on the take with the White Queen, so only share it with people you know are loyal to the Caterpillar. The last thing I want is for this to get back to the White Queen before we can track down Yin."

"I'll do what I can," Aman said, nodding. "And if we get out of this alive, then we'll have a talk."

I smirked. "That almost makes me hope I don't make it out of this alive."

# CHAPTER FORTY-ONE

After following him across the city, I slid into Dormouse's car at the second house on our list. "First place was a bust?"

"I couldn't find any sign of life there, and trust me, I tried. I assume you showing up without backup means we're on our own."

"Afraid so. Captain doesn't think spending half the force's resources on a hunch is a good idea."

"And yet, if we find Yin, he'll take the credit for it."

"Oh, for sure." I looked out at the two-story house we were staked out in front of. It was in worse shape, somehow, than the rowhouse the dealer escaped from earlier. It was clear whoever owned these houses took no pride in their upkeep, giving credence to my theory they were just places to stash people where nobody would look. "How do you want to play it?"

"Now that you're here, I think I go through the front, and you smash through the back. I'll rush up the stairs, and you check the main floor."

"What about probable cause?"

"These places don't exist according to the land records, and yet, here I am, looking at them. If that's not probable cause, I don't know what is."

He was grasping at straws, but I didn't care. I needed to get Yin back to Caterpillar soon to avoid the streets running red with blood, which meant bending the rules well past their breaking point.

"Let's go. I'll whistle when it's go time."

Dormouse rushed up the porch stairs as I made my way past the overgrown weeds and into the back of the house. There was no deck, just a rickety door that hung above a set of stairs. I waited for Dormouse's whistle to indicate it was time to breach.

When he gave the signal, I wedged my shoulder into the door and slammed hard into it. Some doors took more force than others, but this one crumpled for me as my shoulder crashed through the waterlogged material. I pulled my gun out of the holster and started to move room to room as Dormouse's footsteps rushed up the stairs and through the second floor.

"Anything?" I asked, looking up the stairs when he appeared again.

He shook his head. "No, and no sign of anybody staying here."

I moved back to the kitchen and opened the rusted fridge. The light was out, and it was tepid inside with nothing except for a box of moldy baking soda. The cupboards were equally bare, and when I took the stairs down to the basement, I didn't find anything except cobwebs and an abandoned bicycle.

When we moved back outside, a black and white car was stationed across the street. They tipped their hat to me, and I nodded to them. They didn't need to say anything. This was all Aman could do, make sure that once we finished casing a joint, they would be watched by a team he trusted. The side benefit meant I could learn all the people on Caterpillar's payroll, so when I figured out how to take them down, all of them would fall together.

We moved on to the third house and the fourth after that, finding nothing both times, except for a small bag of

Rabbit that had been left over when whoever was staying in the place abandoned it for wherever they ended up next.

At the fifth house, we found a half dozen cars parked in the driveway and the yard. It had fallen to night during our trip to the other houses, and there was clearly a party happening inside.

"This is promising," I said.

"Yeah, but we're only two people. Do you think the captain will send backup, maybe, since we don't want to be overwhelmed by a group of murderous drug dealers?"

"I think it warrants a call to the captain." I made a video call to the captain's cell phone, and he picked up grumpily, barking at me as I flipped the phone around. "This is one of the houses we're checking out. There are a dozen or so people inside. You can make them out from the shadows in the window. It looks like they're having a party. We will get overrun if we take them on ourselves. Can you spare some men now?"

I flipped the phone around to see the captain's ugly mug snarling and stewing. "Give me twenty minutes. I'll get as many squads as I can muster out there."

True to his word, ten squad cars showed up, and within half an hour, twenty-four of us were ready to infiltrate the house. The paddy wagon even showed up and stopped anyone that came down the street, detaining them for questioning in case they would give a clue to the White Queen.

The uniforms took positions around the back of the house while Dormouse and I walked up to the front door. As we did, I noticed a familiar motorcycle on the grass that had been as of yet obscured by an old Buick parked in front of it. "Dormouse, look."

He nodded to me when he saw it. Yin's dealer was inside, which meant maybe there was a chance he was inside, too.

My hand shook as I held my gun up to the door. I had seen my share of these busts in my day, and they never got easier. This time was harder than most because the adrenaline coursing through my blood played hell with my anxiety, and I fought against my body to keep it from collapsing into a puddle on the ground.

"NOW!" Dormouse shouted, and he smashed through the door with his leg. The anxiety abated, giving way to experience, and I pushed into the door after him. The partiers inside the house all screamed as the police funneled in behind me and streamed in from the back of the house.

Their job was to secure the main floor and basement while Dormouse and I snaked through the upstairs, clearing each room. Two patrolmen followed us upstairs. I smashed open the door in front of us to find two men making out in the bathroom.

"OUT!" I shouted. "Downstairs."

They fled, half-naked, down the stairs. Dormouse strafed right to smash through a door there. "There's nothing here. Clear!"

I did the same with two more rooms, clearing them even in the darkness, before meeting Dormouse at the last door. I nodded and he smashed through the room. There was a naked man in the bed, and the window was open. I heard a motorcycle's engine rev from the ground.

"No!" I shouted.

I dove out the window and saw the dealer spinning her motorcycle to disappear into the night. Not this time. I leaped off the roof and landed on her back, slamming her to the ground as the motorcycle shot out from under her. I rolled over and pulled her hands behind her back.

"Got you. Now, where's Yin?"

# CHAPTER FORTY-TWO

The dealer laughed, long and hard, as I dug my knee deeper into her back.

"What's so funny?"

She dropped her head back until it was hanging loose. "You have no idea what you're doing, do you?"

"I have some ideas, but clarify for me." I shook her until her head flopped forward and caught my eyes. "What specifically are you talking about?"

"There is a reckoning coming," she said with a smile. Her teeth were capped with a gold grill. "And it's going to change everything."

I pulled her close to me. "I don't give a shit about your cryptic bull. Just tell me where Yin is, and I'll go easy on you."

"It doesn't matter. He's already gone, man. Don't you get it? He doesn't matter. None of us matter. We're just fodder for the coming war. Foot soldiers in a war of attrition."

"Did you kill him? Is he dead?" My words were getting more frantic. "Tell me!"

"Liddell!" Dormouse barked. "Let her go."

"Yeah, Detective," she whispered to me. "Let me go. It's unseemly to beg in public."

"You're going to jail for a long time." I pulled out my gun and aimed it at her. "Now, tell me what you know, and maybe I can go easy on you. Otherwise—"

"You don't scare me. You have no idea who you're messing with." She smiled. "I'll be dead by morning now. You can count on that, and I don't fucking care."

"You can't want to die."

"I didn't choose to live. Why should I care if I die? Let me ask you, Detective, if you could choose to exist, would you? If somebody could make it all end, would you let them take it from you, so you could end all this bullshit?"

"I don't care about any of your nihilistic rambling." I cocked the gun. "I'll give you one last chance."

"That's the difference between us, I guess. You would do anything to live, and I would do anything to die."

Dormouse pulled me off the girl, but I struggled against him. "I'm not done! Stop—let me go, gods da—"

"Enough," Dormouse said. "We're not criminals. You can't threaten a prisoner. What's wrong with you?"

I knew exactly what was wrong with me. I was fighting against time to stop an all-out war between Caterpillar and his enemies, but I still couldn't tell Dormouse any of that.

"Don't let her out of your sight," I said to an officer who slapped cuffs on her. "She's planning something, and I don't know what it is. And station extra guards on her cell when you get her to jail."

My phone rang, and I opened it to find Aman's voice barking at me. "Did you find him? Or did I waste my resources?"

"We found the dealer we were looking for, but no sign of Yin. We think he's fled town already. They said he's gone."

"Not good enough, Detective Liddell. We can't bring that back to our mutual friend and get him to call off his squad."

"We just took down a huge chunk of the White Queen's operation, Captain. That has to count for something."

"I'm sure it does, but not enough. Keep looking. You can stop when you've found him, or you're dead, whichever comes first."

"Detective!" an officer called from the house as I hung up the phone. "You need to come listen to this."

I walked past the woman and into the house. Most of the dealers were silent, kneeling on the ground, keeping their mouths shut, but in the back, there was one, a young man with a shaved head, except for one twirl of purple in the center of it, babbling on the ground.

"I don't want to die. I don't want to die."

The uniform pointed to him. "This one keeps babbling about something."

I knelt in front of him. "You have something to tell me, boy?"

He nodded. "I'll tell you what you want to know, but you have to get me out of here right now!"

"Shut up!" one of the other partiers said, an older man with a bushy beard.

"NO! I'm not a pawn!" he screamed before turning to me. "I'll show you where we took Yin, but you can't—we can't be here. You have no idea what she's going to do."

"Fine," I replied. "We'll get you out of here, but you better have something for me."

"I do," he said when I pulled him up. "I swear I do."

"If you show us where Yin is, I'll do what I can to keep you safe. You have my word."

"And is your word good?"

I shrugged. "That's all I have. Otherwise, I'll leave you here to whatever fate you fear."

He nodded. "Okay, fine. I'll show you. I'll tell you, just please—you have to get me out of here now."

"Fine." I pushed him forward. "Then start walking."

As we walked, the dealers around started to growl, calling him a traitor and threatening to break him in half, but he didn't respond. He was too busy crying and blubbering to himself. When we were outside, the girl who I arrested looked up at us and sneered.

"I knew we should never have brought you in, coward."

"I—I'm sorry."

She kicked out her feet and tripped him. It was only me grabbing him by the back and pulling him up that prevented him from slamming his nose on the idling bike.

Before we got into my car, I threw the boy onto the hood. "Now, how do I know you're not going to lead me into a trap?"

"I'm not like them, man. They are crazy. They don't give a shit about anything except bringing Wonderland back to chaos. I'm not—I was just trying to make some money. I thought—I thought it would be like the other gangs, man. I thought maybe I'd get jumped in and have to pledge loyalty, but they are fucking nuts. The things they want you to do—they will die for her, man, and I just—I don't want that life."

"Nobody is that crazy."

"They will die for her, man. They will do anything not to disappoint her."

I thought back to the words the dealer I arrested told me, that she would rather die than live in captivity—that she didn't value her life—and the boy's words seemed to track with that. If they were all as crazy as her, it would be hard to break them.

"Stop!" I heard somebody behind me.

I turned to see that the woman dealer had escaped her handler and rushed to the house.

"I will see you in the hereafter, brothers!" she screamed as she reached the porch.

She slammed her leg against a pipe against the house, and then, a second later, the whole place exploded, sending us flying backward, as the mushroom cloud plumed into the air, taking the house, and all the officers inside, with it.

# CHAPTER FORTY-THREE

I thought the White Queen wasn't ready for a war, but now I knew that wasn't the case. She wasn't only planning for war, she was counting on it and had been training foot soldiers so loyal they would gladly die for her.

Every one of the men that the captain sent was on the take from Caterpillar, and in one fell swoop, she took down twenty of his men. Yes, just as many of her own were taken in the process, but they were low-level thugs, not narcs. We took their pawns. She took our knights. Any chess player would take that gambit any day of the week.

I opened my eyes and coughed smoke out of my lungs. The punk kid lay under me, cushioning my fall. He groaned as I rolled off of him.

"You knew!" I shouted, grabbing the boy by the jacket. "You knew, and you said nothing!"

"I'm sorry, I'm sorry. If I said any more, they would have—I couldn't—I'm sorry, but I couldn't—"

I kicked him back down. "Stay there, or I'll fucking kill you."

"I will, I will, I will," he kept muttering, curled up in a ball as the world burned around him.

"DORMOUSE!" I shouted, rushing into the street to find him.

"Ow," he said achingly.

"Are you okay?"

He pushed himself to stand. "I think so."

We walked over to the punk kid together. I grabbed him by his scruff and pulled him to stand. "How did she know? How did the White Queen know we would come?"

"I don't know! I don't know! We didn't even know until we got there, and then that crazy bitch said we couldn't leave until you came, and then she rushed off. I thought it was just a lark, you know, but when we passed her—I knew."

I let go of his collar. The dealer I leaped onto from the roof had been trying to leave. If she was going to leave, she couldn't have meant to—unless there was a detonator. I thought I saw something slide out from her jacket when I tackled her, but I assumed it was nothing important and that if it was, we had time to search for it.

I left the punk with Dormouse and walked toward the wreckage of the house. The fire still raged, and there was debris everywhere, but I picked it up, scouring for something, anything, until I found it. Buried among the broken boards and discarded glass was a small receiver with a single red button in the middle, mangled in the blast, but it certainly looked like a detonator of some type. She was planning on leaving and blowing the place up with me inside, with all of us inside, the people who got closest to finding her.

I grabbed an evidence bag out of my trunk and wrapped the detonator in it. Then I walked back to my car. "Come on."

"Where are you going?" Dormouse asked.

"We still have to find Yin."

"There are more important things to do."

I pushed the punk into my car and slammed the door behind him. "Maybe for you, but I still have to stop a gang war. You don't need me here anymore."

"Our comrades died," Dormouse said, tears in his eyes. "And you're acting like you don't care at all."

"I can't care," I said, slamming my door closed and starting the car. "Otherwise, I'll fall apart, and I have to end this before it gets worse."

It didn't matter if it was a trap. I already survived one today, and if I died going into another, it would be my just desserts. I trusted the bookkeeper in City Hall and the surveillance tech, but they could have easily been on the White Queen's payroll, or the dealer who escaped could have told the White Queen what happened, and she could have set this all up to catch us. Whatever the reason, now it was personal.

"Where are we going, kid?"

"William," he replied. "Edge of the city. Chesterfield Forest. We should stop by and pick up a shovel first."

That was all I needed to hear to know Yin was dead, and an hour later, my suspicions were confirmed when I watched William dig up the shallow grave and unveil his dead body in the dirt.

"Bring it with you," I said, swallowing what remained of my emotion.

He pulled Yin's dead body out of the hole they dug for him and stuffed him in the trunk of my car. When I slammed the trunk closed, I turned to him.

"Did you kill him?" I asked. "And don't fucking lie to me."

He shook his head. "Nah, man. He was dead when I got to the house. They needed another person to help dig the grave, and that's all I did. You do some fucked up shit when you work for the White Queen, but I would never kill a kid."

"I don't believe that at all, William. I think our morals are flexible. You might say you would never kill somebody today, but in a week, a month, or a year, as you fell further and further down the rabbit hole, who knows what you would do?"

I was talking to myself as much as I was talking to William, giving myself a warning about how far I could fall if I kept searching down this particular rabbit hole, working for the Caterpillar, digging up dirt on the White Queen. How many more people would have to die before it was all over? And would I live to see the end?

It didn't matter because I was ready to see this out until the end, even if it killed me. Hell, maybe, especially if it killed me, but make no mistake. I didn't choose to be born, but I would fight like hell to live and bring the White Queen to justice.

"Let's go, Billy," I grumbled. "We still have more to do."

"Are you going to take me to jail?"

I shook my head. "They can't protect you. We can't protect you. We can't even protect our own people. No, there's only one place you might be safe now, and there's just as good a chance he'll kill you." His eyes went wide. "Don't worry, Billy. I'll put in a good word for you. Who knows? It just might mean something."

# CHAPTER FORTY-FOUR

William stayed silent all the way to the Looking Glass. When I walked in, Caterpillar was railing furiously at a group of goons ten deep. Many were still fully human, but there was also a rat and two tigers, along with a bonobo monkey in the mix as well, holding automatic rifles and staring up at their boss as he stormed across the stage.

"Whe're ghoing to rip their guts out, dho yhou understand me an—" His eyes found me in the crowd. "Ah, Detective, whe have eagerly been anticipating yhour arrival. Now, yhou get to see the fhinal act of this play."

"Hold the curtains, Caterpillar. We found Yin."

His eyes narrowed. "This has ghone whay past the poor, unfortunate bhoy."

I pushed young William forward. "Then listen to what this boy has to say about the White Queen." We had practiced his speech all the way over here, but now he was frozen with all eyes focused on him. "Go on, Billy. They're waiting, and Caterpillar doesn't like waiting."

"She's right, Bhilly. If yhou have something to say, nhow is the thime."

He swallowed. "The White Queen…she wants you to come at her. I don't know her plan, but whatever it is, the worst thing you can do is chase after her right now."

"Ahre yhou one of her boys, Billy?" His voice was menacing. "Dhid yhou help kill my men?"

"He was at the party," I said. "But he's a cog in a much bigger machine. The White Queen people, they are crazy. I watched them willingly die for her just to spite you."

"Ahll the more rheason to take her down now, before she ghets bigger."

I stepped forward. "And where are you going to search for her? Are you going to flip over every table until you luck out? Even the NARCOs can't help you if you go rogue like that. You have to understand, she wants you to burn your bridges with the NARCOs, so they have no choice but to take you down."

"Ahnd, what do you suggest?" He stopped pacing.

"Let me look into it for you. I'll get Billy's statement, and he'll help me however he can." I looked over at him. "Won't you, Billy?"

"I will, yes I will, Mr. Caterpillar." He nodded furiously. "Whatever you need."

"This injustice cannot stand," Caterpillar growled. "If I let him live—"

"Then what? Do you think killing a little kid, a pawn in this game, is going to do anything to restore your reputation?" I stepped forward. "Think about it. He was supposed to die in that explosion, yet we got him. He lived. I was supposed to die in that explosion, same with Dormouse. Whatever plan the White Queen has, it needed all three of us to be out of the way, which means we put a wrench in her gears. She'll have to step back, rethink, and replan. If you don't attack, and the NARCOs don't come down on you, then she has to replan even more. Don't fall into her trap because you let emotions get the best of you."

"Yhou make a fhair point." He sneered at me for a moment before taking a break and catching himself. "Where is the bhoy? Where is Yin?"

I dropped my eyes. "He's dead. Billy didn't have a hand in killing him, but he did lead me to his body. The only reason we have Yin back is because of him."

Caterpillar hopped down from the stage and over to Billy. "Is that true? Are yhou a hero, Billy?"

He shook his head. "No, a hero would have saved his life. I didn't do that. I'm trying to help now, though. I don't want to die, and I know if I go back to the White Queen, that's what's gonna happen, and if I run, she'll find me. I got nowhere else to go except hoping you'll take pity on me."

"And yhou whant me to take pity on yhou?"

"Yes, sir. I can help you. I don't know much, but anything I know I'll use to help you find the White Queen."

"Yhes, yhou whill." He snapped his fingers, and two of his men jumped toward him. "Ghet poor Yin from the detective's char, whill yhou?" He looked at me. "Keys?"

I tossed my keys to the bigger of the two, who was halfway through a transformation into a rat, and they rushed out.

"So, what now? Are you still going to raze this city to the ground?"

He gritted his teeth. "I think nhot yhet. There are too mhany factors I dhon't understand. I thought the White Queen whas another poser, bhut it seems she is more fhormitable than I anticipated." He moved toward me, stroking my cheek with the back of his clammy hand. "However, if this ghets out of control, then yhou whill pay the price, my dhear. Yhou and yhour perfect fhamily."

I snapped my arm up and ripped his hand from my cheek. "If you ever threaten my sister or her family again, I will kill you where you stand. Do you understand?"

He sneered, pulling his hand away. I could have held it longer, but I let him keep his pride. After all, he had so little of it left. "Yhou are no fhun!"

I turned to the door to see the two soldiers pull in Yin's body. "I have to go and try to clean up this mess. I'll be in touch."

He wrapped his arm around William. "Nhot if weeee are in touch fhirst."

# CHAPTER FORTY-FIVE

I averted a war, but I still had a mess to clean up with Aman. The scathing looks came from every corner when I entered the station. The uniforms always hated me, but now it was everyone from the janitors to the secretaries that stared at me with malice. It was my operation. I called the narcs to the scene, yet I walked away unharmed while their brothers and sisters died in the explosion. It didn't take a genius to hear what they were thinking.

*It should have been me.*

And I didn't disagree with them. It would have been a whole lot easier if I died earlier tonight. Maybe there would have been a gang war, but I wouldn't have had to deal with it. I would be dead, at peace. Wouldn't that be nice?

"Get in here, Liddell," Aman growled at me as I walked into the bullpen. The eyes were no less kind than they were downstairs, and the worst fire came from Aman's eyes. I entered the office, and he locked the door behind me. The curtains were still drawn from our last encounter.

"This is fucked, all of it," he said. "Do you know what a shitshow this has become? First, you kill a kid, then you pull it from the brink and get a medal, only to be doused with paint. Then you make up with the mother and nearly solve the case, only to fail to properly case the house for explosives and send twenty-two of our officers to their graves."

"I'm so sorry," I said. "I didn't know. Who would have thought—"

"A good cop would have checked."

I swallowed the tears forming in my eyes. "No offense, but there were twenty-four narcs at that house tonight, and none of them looked for a bomb. It's not protocol, and—"

"Don't try to weasel out of this, Liddell. You are in a mountain of shit, and no amount of digging can pull you out of it."

I bit my lip. "Did you give this same speech to Dormouse? Or am I special?"

"He's still at the scene, Liddell, but you left it. Why?"

I looked up at him, catching his bloodshot eyes. "I had to find Yin and bring him to our boss before he lit the whole city on fire looking for the White Queen. I weep for those officers, but they would stay dead no matter what action I took. What I did saved a whole lot of lives."

"It doesn't look that way. It looks like you are a coward."

"Then you can call Caterpillar and—"

"It won't matter. I can't take the word of a criminal— you're being reassigned uptown. The top brass knows they can't fire you without bringing down a shitstorm on us, but we're hoping we can put you in a sleepy little precinct where nobody knows you and let things calm down here."

"I didn't do anything wrong!" I shouted.

Aman blew angry fire out of his nose. "We both know that's not true. This might not all be your fault, but you did plenty wrong, not the least of which being that you got caught up with Caterpillar in the first place."

"That means half the station is in the wrong then, right?"

He turned from me and took a seat at his desk. "We're all in the wrong, every one of us. All we can do is try to keep our noses clean and clean up our messes. Even if I wanted to fight for you, I couldn't. This comes from up high."

"And what does Caterpillar think about that?"

Aman's eyes narrowed. "You assaulted him tonight and made him look like a fool in front of his men. You're lucky he doesn't kill you where you stand, but for some reason, he has an affection for you." He signed some papers on his desk. "You can still look into the White Queen from uptown, but don't show your face in this precinct ever again. Otherwise, I can't—"

"You can't what?"

"I can't guarantee your safety. I've already had to suspend two officers for threatening to slice your throat." He sighed. "You're a good cop in a spiral. Take two weeks off, then report to precinct 14 for reassignment."

"Please, Captain. Don't do this."

He looked up at me. "I couldn't help you even if I liked you. Since I don't, I won't even try. Now get out. You're no longer my concern."

# EPILOGUE

*Wonderland.*

Dark. Grimy. Unsavory.

It didn't use to be this way. It used to be a place to forget all your problems and get lost in the fantasy of your life. I never understood that until I inhaled Rabbit and got lost in the madness myself. When I returned to reality, everything fell apart, and suddenly, I got it. I understood exactly why somebody would choose to fall into oblivion than deal with the world.

I already knew where to get Rabbit. That was something every NARCO knew. The dirty little secret. Rabbit was everywhere.

"What do you want?" A hog-nose morpher stood in front of me. We were alone in a dark alley; the same alley where I once shot a kid. It didn't take long for them to set up a new system, and luckily the pig-faced dealer didn't recognize me. I would never forget him.

"Give me a hit," I said.

He pulled a vial out of his coat. "Five grand."

I pulled my badge out of my pocket. "Let's just keep this our little secret, and we'll call it even." I thought for a second. "In fact, better make it two."

*

You have finished reading *White Rabbit*. If you enjoyed this book, make sure to keep reading after the author notes for a sneak peak at the second book in the duology, *Black Jack.*

# AUTHOR NOTES

I wrote the first 10,000 (okay, 11,000) words of this story back in 2017 when I had no idea what I wanted to be as a writer. I had an inkling about fantasy, or horror, or…well, I just didn't know for sure what kind of story I liked to tell, but this idea sprang into my head almost fully formed, and I decided to take the time to write the first part about chasing the bunny and finding him. Being on heroin is called "chasing the dragon," and I thought it was appropriate to have her both figuratively and literally chasing the bunny as she chased down Rabbit in the city.

It was really, really hard blending my voice from 2017 with my voice in 2021. For instance, I used a lot of scene breaks back in 2017 and have since stopped using them nearly as much, preferring shorter chapters or blending transitions better than I knew how to do back then. I had to go back during editing and fix all that for this story. I took the first seven chapters and broke them up into ten to make it read correctly with the rest of the book.

My management team has been hounding me to make this book since they found out about the concept, and I would be lying if part of my reason for writing it wasn't to make them happy and to make my wife happy by using some of the covers that I bought all the way back in 2018. However, finally being able to finish this book made me happy, too. Thrillers are not my main genre, but The Godsverse Chronicles, my big mythological fantasy action-adventure series, follow a thriller formula at their core, except with magic, monsters, mythology, and jumping around the universe. It was fun to strip all of that away and just focus on the thriller part without the magic.

Part of what scared me about writing this book for so long was that the reviews of the first part were mixed. Either people LOVED it or HATED it, and it has traditionally been my worst reviewed singular story, and I didn't know if that meant I should never write it or that I should dive in. After all, the people who loved it REALLY LOVED it.

Since finishing The Godsverse Chronicles earlier in 2021, I have been looking for a new long-term project, and just like I did back in 2018 when I wrote *The Marked Ones, Invasion, Anna and The Dark Place,* and *The Void Calls Us Home* searching for The Obsidian Spindle Saga, I thought it would be good to do that again and clear out some of the backlog of covers I've had for so long. I started with *Dragon Strife*, my epic fantasy novel series, and now I'm working on this series between stints on *The Obsidian Spindle Saga.* I have one other series to write after this as I search for the next thing, and I'm hoping by the time I finish this trilogy and my next one, I'll know what I want to do next because right now, I'm just not sure.

It's a weird place to be as a writer, especially if you are me because, since 2017, I have always known at least the current big thing and the next big thing, but in 2022 I'm finishing *Cthulhu is Hard to Spell, Ichabod Jones: Monster Hunter, The Godsverse Chronicles,* and will finish writing (though not releasing *The Obsidian Spindle Saga*). These are the series that have dominated my career, and it is legit scary that I don't even have an inkling of an idea.

No, that's not true, I do have an inkling, but it's a distant point on the horizon I can't grasp. I'm hoping that this series will bring me closer to it, especially because it's so different than anything I've ever done before.

Even when I wrote *Invasion,* I had written a lot of science fiction before, whereas this feels like it's coming out of left field. I haven't written a true thriller since 2008, when I wrote the movie script *Vengeance,* which didn't go anywhere but was the first thing I had optioned.

It felt good to get back in the saddle. It's weird to not be able to rely on magic to move the story along, but most stories are just two people walking into a room and talking, which means that the foundations of this book are similar to my others.

After so long in development, I'm very happy I could deliver on the promise I gave so many years ago to finish this book, and if you liked it, I hope you'll join me in *Black Jack,* the second book in this trilogy, where we explore Alice Liddell falling even farther down the rabbit hole as she descends into the madness of Wonderland, and the CARDs gang, which have begun muscling in on Caterpillar's turf after the events in this book.

*

Now, here's a sneak peek at *Black Jack.*

# BLACK JACK

## Book 2 of the Wonderland duology

By:

Russell Nohelty

Edited by:

Jonas Saul

Proofread by:

Lily Luchesi

Toni Cox

Cover by:

Paramita Bhattacharjee

# CHAPTER ONE

I hated myself for saying it, but being transferred to a sleepy department north of Wonderland wasn't all terrible. I thought I would miss the high-stakes life or death action of the 91st precinct, but it absolutely was not the worst thing that ever happened to me, even if it stemmed from the worst thing that ever happened to me.

My sister Dinah took my timidity in bashing everything about my new boss as a tacit agreement that she was right the whole time about me moving to the suburbs, but not hating every second of my life was a far cry from falling in love with the slower pace. Perhaps Dinah loathed her new life so deeply that she forgot enjoyment and hatred were two different emotions.

That would explain quite a lot about my sister, actually, and the constant bickering about my choices that created the din of my relationship with her.

"Are you coming to dinner tonight?" she asked as we stood in the butcher line at the H.E.B., an enormous, pristine grocery store very different from the grimy bodegas I used to frequent. She filled a whole cart and part of another (that she forced me to push) for a single week of cooking. Meanwhile, everything I ate fit in a single basket and consisted mostly of coffee and vodka, with a couple of TV dinners thrown in for good measure (and so my sister would not get on my case about eating out every meal).

"It's Friday, isn't it?" I asked. "That's the tradition."

"Well, it's a new tradition," she replied. "Usually, you had a case that prevented you from coming over, or something always came up."

I sucked my teeth. "Yeah, about half of those were complete lies."

"Only half?" she asked with a chipper smile. "I figured as much, but I'm surprised you are so forthright about it."

"Forthright is my new MO, sis."

"That's nice. I like that." She looked down at my basket disapprovingly. "Now, we just have to teach you to cook."

"I know how to cook," I replied. "That's why I don't wanna do it."

"Arthur is not going to stay with you long if you don't learn how to feed him."

Arthur was my boyfriend. He worked as a journalist, which meant he kept the same awful hours as me and didn't mind when I blew him off for a case, and I didn't mind when he had a late deadline. We met up, had our fun, and went our separate ways. It was about the only type of relationship I was capable of at the moment, and I wasn't looking to get any more serious than what we had.

Sometimes, I could tell he wanted more, but then a case would break for me, or he would get a scoop, and the tension would break. Once, we had a long enough conversation to warrant a pregnant pause, which led to a long silence. It was the kind of silence that was usually filled with professions of love or deep questions about the future, but when he opened his mouth to speak, I defused the situation by sticking my tongue in it, and all was well.

"I don't need to feed him. I just have to fuck him, and while I'm a hell of a screw-up, I am a master in the bedroom." I smirked at her. "Maybe you should try that instead of spending all day in the kitchen."

"Excuse me!" Dinah said with an exasperated scoff. "We have two kids, and I can guarantee you they didn't come from a stork."

"Sure," I replied. "But when was the last time you guys had sex?"

Dinah shrugged. "I guess it's been a while, but we're very busy, both of us."

"Sure, sure. I mean, I get it. I just wish you got it, too."

"That is a very gross wish," she replied. "Please stop wishing about my sex life."

The conversation about my sister's bedroom activities was mercifully cut short when the butcher called our number, and we placed our order. Dinah needed a pot roast to put in the crock pot before she went to work, and I had the day off, and idle hands were a devil's plaything.

Once we were finished, Dinah walked to her car, and I went to mine. She had picked up a job at a real estate office in the afternoons to keep her own idle hands busy, and I brought myself home to put my meager groceries in the fridge.

I stayed in my old place, even though the move would save thirty minutes and two subway transfers. It was part the habit, part the metal door my old department installed to prevent protesters from ripping me apart, and part because I hoped that my old department would come to their senses and bring me back to vice. Of course, that part of me wasn't stupid. You can't send twenty officers into a trap that got them killed and not expect there to be consequences.

I couldn't even go to their funerals and pay my respects. The police commissioner literally told me I would be fired and arrested if I showed up within five hundred feet of any of their families, and he wasn't messing around.

Even Caterpillar couldn't bring me back into their good graces.

After putting away my groceries, I flopped onto the couch, hoping to get some sleep, but dreading it at the same time. Sleep meant dreams, and that's when the charred bodies of the narcs I led to their deaths haunted me.

I closed my eyes, but the screaming, charred zombies of my fellow officers I sent to their deaths jolted me awake. It haunted me in the quiet moments, preventing me from getting a moment's peace for many, many months. Since I couldn't sleep, I pulled out my phone and texted Arthur.

*Me: Come over.*

*Him: Working.*

*Me: Now.*

*Him:...*

*Him: I'll be right there.*

*Me: Damn right.*

I smirked and put away my phone. You absolutely didn't have to cook for your man if you could fuck him into oblivion. If you could do that, they would answer your beck and call like a horny little puppy.

# CHAPTER TWO

After Arthur was done satisfying me, he rolled off my chest and let out a deep, contented sigh. I turned to him and smiled. "So, was it worth blowing your scoop?"

He laughed. "There will be another one. Besides, these press conferences are always a bore. I'll call my buddy and get the details before the deadline."

He didn't answer my question. He was always evasive like that. He couldn't give me a simple yes or no answer, and it frustrated me to no end. "So…"

He caught my eye for a second before shaking his head. "You really are a needy dame; did you know that?"

"Rude." I scoffed and hit him with one of my pillows as I stood and walked to the bathroom. "Who says things like that? What are you, a reporter from the twenties? Do you have one of those bills in the brim of your derby?"

There was a beat of silence as he thought about it. "But dear, I literally am a reporter from the twenties."

Grr. He was right. "The 2020s was not what I meant, and you know it."

"You're a cop, Alice. You, of all people, should know the value of being precise, especially to a reporter."

I closed the door to the bathroom for some privacy. He was annoying, especially in the way he always had to be right, but it was nice to match wits with somebody again. Most of the men I slept with were barely good for three pumps and a grunt before they lost their value to me. For all the aggravation he caused, Arthur kept things interesting.

"Hey," he asked when I was finally done in the bathroom. "Why do girls always pee after sex?"

I looked at him foolishly. "Are you serious?"

"Why?" he replied, cocking his head. "Is that a stupid question?"

"Well, you're a thirty-year-old man who has been sexually active for at least a couple of months, and you're a reporter, so I figured you would know."

He shrugged. "I never really thought about it."

I walked over to the dresser to grab a new pair of underwear so I could take a shower and prepare for dinner with the family. "You ask questions about every little thing in the universe, and you never thought to ask about that?"

He furrowed his brow. "It never came up."

"You have a computer, a phone, and a database at work with thousands of experts at your disposal. Look it up."

He sat up. "Yeah, but I'm asking you."

"It's a very sexy question, my friend."

"I'm not trying to be sexy. I was just trying to have a conversation. Seriously, you think I'm frustrating? How about how you aggressively refuse to answer even the smallest question?"

"I'm not refusing to answer," I replied, taking off my shirt. "I'm just agog at the fact you don't know your dick is filled with bacteria, and if I don't pee, I'll get a UTI. I don't know if you've ever had one of them, but they aren't pleasant."

"Hrm." He seemed pensive. "That makes sense. Do you have to poop after butt stuff?"

"I'm not having this conversation." I walked back to the bathroom. "You need to go, or I'll be late for dinner."

He hopped off the bed. "When are you going to invite me to your sister's house? We've been together for a while now."

"As fuck buddies, and nothing more." I laughed. "Never. You will never, ever meet my family."

His face dropped. "Oh."

I threw my clothes on the counter and turned on the shower. "Does that upset you?"

"Well, yeah. I thought maybe this was going somewhere, but if I'm never going to meet your family, then it means—"

This was the conversation I was trying to avoid. I turned off the water because it was about to get awkward, and I didn't want to waste a month's worth of water while I had a fight with the person I was sleeping with.

"That's exactly what it means," I said. "And you know I don't want to talk about this."

"But I do. Doesn't that count for something?"

"Absolutely not. This isn't going Dutch on a pizza. You don't have that conversation just to appease the other person. It's like sex. If one person doesn't want to have it, you don't force it on them, or you're an asshole."

"So, I'm an asshole now?" There was scorn in his voice.

"Oh my god, you are such an asshole, but until this moment, the kind of asshole which was charming in their way. Now, you're just being the annoying type of asshole."

He threw on his pants. "I didn't know it was annoying to want to be around you, to want to grow closer to you."

"Have you met me?" My eyebrows furrowed. "Getting emotional is about the most annoying thing you could ever do to me, and getting close to me means sharing emotions. No, thank you."

"You're a real bitch, you know that?"

"Yes!" I shouted enthusiastically. "I am absolutely aware I'm hard to love and harder to like. I know I'm complicated and messed up, but that's who I am. If you don't like it, then you can see yourself to the door." I turned on the water again. "And if you're not okay with being around my particular brand of crazy, you don't have to come back."

"That's not—"

"If you do, though, then know this is as much as I can give. It's the most I want to give. I'm not going to change, and I don't want to change. I don't want you to stay around because you think I'll somehow mend myself together and become a whole, real person in a year or two because that's not going to happen, and you're wasting your time."

I closed the door to the bathroom and locked it behind me. I heard Arthur bang on the door as I stepped into the shower, but I wasn't about to let him in. I didn't want him to see me cry, and the shower drowned out my whimpering. I bit my lip until the noise finally stopped, and I heard him walk to the front door and slam it behind him.

Why was I like this? Arthur was a fine person who seemed to genuinely like me. The most annoying thing about him was that he wanted to spend time with me and get to know me better. That wasn't so bad, was it? Then why did it feel like being stabbed with a hot knife every time he opened his mouth?

I finished my shower and dried myself off. I didn't look at myself in the mirror much anymore, and I stopped wearing makeup completely. People always said the natural look was in, but I still got plenty of looks when I went places like I was a pasty, hot mess that could do with a pound of foundation to cover the bags under my eyes and blotchy skin.

By the time I finished dressing and getting myself ready, it was well past the time I should have left. Luckily, I had a squad car that wasn't due back until tomorrow and had no problem running lights to speed my way through the city.

My phone buzzed when I went to pick it up, and my heart dropped when I saw the text. It was from Caterpillar. I hadn't heard from him in months.

*I need to see you. Get to the club. Now.*

Well, I guess I'm not seeing my sister tonight after all.

*

If you liked this preview, make sure to buy *Black Jack* today.

# ALSO BY RUSSELL NOHELTY

**THE OBSIDIAN SPINDLE SAGA**
The Sleeping Beauty
The Wicked Witch
The Fairy Queen
The Red Rider
**THE GODVERSE CHRONICLES**
And Death Followed Behind Her
And Doom Followed Behind Her
And Ruin Followed Behind Her
And Hell Followed Behind Her
And Conquest Followed Behind Them
And Darkness Followed Behind Her
And Chaos Followed Behind Them
Katrina Hates the Dead
Pixie Dust
**OTHER NOVEL WORK**
My Father Didn't Kill Himself
Sorry for Existing
Gumshoes: The Case of Madison's Father
The Invasion Saga
The Vessel
Worst Thing in the Universe
The Void Calls Us Home
The Marked Ones
**OTHER ILLUSTRATED WORK**
The Little Bird and the Little Worm
Ichabod Jones: Monster Hunter
Gherkin Boy
**www.russellnohelty.com**